POWER OF
Discovery

C. Blaine Hyatt, M.S.
and
Linda Lee Hyatt, Ph.D.

Power of Discovery

Copyright © 2023 by Blaine Hyatt, M.S. and Linda Lee Hyatt, Ph.D. All rights reserved.

No part of this publication may be reproduced, stored in a retrieval system or transmitted in any way by any means, electronic, mechanical, photocopy, recording or otherwise without the prior permission of the author except as provided by USA copyright law.

The opinions expressed by the author are not necessarily those of URLink Print and Media.

1603 Capitol Ave., Suite 310 Cheyenne, Wyoming USA 82001
1-888-980-6523 | admin@urlinkpublishing.com

URLink Print and Media is committed to excellence in the publishing industry.

Book design copyright © 2023 by URLink Print and Media. All rights reserved.

Published in the United States of America

Library of Congress Control Number: 2023924003
ISBN 978-1-68486-651-9 (Paperback)
ISBN 978-1-68486-652-6 (Digital)

05.12.23

Contents

I Can Sleep When the Wind Blows 1
We are always teaching something 11
Eagle or Chicken 19
What if 23
Hauling Wood 31
Fairness, Favoritism and Equal Treatment 39
Rage 51
It's Lonely at the Top 55
I Want What I Want 61
The Dragonfly Syndrome 67
The Goose in the Wind 71
Any Better Than the Ants 77
The Power of Apology 83
The Greatest Battle Ever Fought 91
Just Short Of The Mark 97

I Can Sleep When the Wind Blows

There is a story told about a farmer who needed to hire a full-time farmhand to assist with the farm work and care of the animals. The farmer advertised and searched for a qualified worker, but found none. One day a young man came to the farmer's house asking for a job. As the farmer talked with this young man, he asked about his qualifications to do farm work and care for the animals. The young man answered, "I can sleep when the wind blows." The farmer was puzzled by this answer and thought, what kind of a qualification can that be? The farmer was not particularly impressed with the young man and to say the least, was baffled by the strange answer, "I can sleep when the wind blows." However, he needed help badly, so he hired the young man.

Days passed, the young man proved to be a good worker and things went well. From time to time the farmer would reflect on the young man's strange statement, "I can sleep when the wind blows." He often thought to himself that this young man is a good worker, he has many qualifications for this kind of work, why did he give only one strange meaningless answer to such an important question when asking for a job?

One night a vicious storm suddenly burst throughout the area. Ferocious winds beat upon the farmer's house, barn, and sheds. Tree limbs crashed to the ground, rain fell in sheets as though great waves were heaving beyond the boundaries of the sea. Large hail pounded like shotgun pellets threatening to injure or destroy anything in its path. Thunder and lightning filled the night sky.

In the midst of this fury, the farmer awakened from a deep sleep and fear clutched his entire being. His heart pounded hard in his chest, his breath came deep and fast as he thought of his barns, buildings, gates and animals being brutally attacked by the uncontrollable elements of nature. Quickly he ran to the young man's bedroom. "Wake up, wake up," he shouted, but there was no response. Reaching the bed, he shook the young man again shouting, "Wake up, it is an emergency. There is a terrible storm. We must take care of the animals and buildings." The young man, being somewhat awake by this time, murmured, "It will be OK," turned over, pulled the covers tightly around his neck, snuggled down into his warm cozy bed and fell into a deep peaceful sleep.

The farmer was furious. How can this young man be so non-caring and insensitive! In anger and frustration, the farmer ran from the house, fighting the vicious wind and battling blinding gales of the storm, he made his way to the barn, only to find that the doors were firmly secured, all the animals were shut safely in the stalls with clean, soft bedding of straw and resting peacefully. Leaving the barn, the farmer made his way through his property and found everything in proper order. The equipment was put away, the gates were closed and securely fastened, and the tarps were all firmly tied. Everything was in order and prepared for any storm that might arise. After finding all to be well and taken care of, the farmer made his way back to the house. Now he understood the young man's answer, "I can sleep when the wind blows."

I had a personal experience not long ago that really drove this principle home. My wife and I decided to add a large family room and eating area onto our home. We had worked on it for about a year and a half and it was almost finished. We had removed a large sliding glass door between the house and the addition. The problem was that the only heat we had in the addition was a wood burning stove which we planned to use in the future for emergencies such as power outages. We planned to put in a gas fireplace for our main heat source. Since the fireplace had not yet been installed, we were using the wood burning stove to heat the addition. It had been an unusually warm and dry winter. We had not had storm for months. The temperatures had been running as high as the 60s and 70s. It had been so warm that we had not even started a fire for days and when we did, it would only be for a few hours.

In the back of our property, there are a bunch of dead trees that have been piled up which I use for our wood source. I would take my chain saw, saw a few blocks of wood and bring them to the house to use as needed. Day after day went by and every few days, I would go get a little wood for a quick fire in the early morning or late evening to take off the chill. As I said, the weather was so warm that getting a supply of wood was not a big deal. Now I knew someday the weather would change, it would get cold and the storms would come. I would often think that I need to sharpen my saw and get some wood in, but I will do it tomorrow. Day after day, I procrastinated. The truth is, I had plenty of time, but I felt tired and just didn't feel like getting wood in, even though I could have. Some days there would be a program on TV that I would watch, not that I needed to. Other times, I sat around, talked and just kind of wasted time. Time was not a reason or an excuse. I just chose to put it off and wait.

The day finally came, as I knew it would. A winter storm was on its way. I could not get wood when I heard of the coming storm, as I had to go to work. By the time I got home from work that day, the storm had arrived. The temperature had begun to drop, a cold rain with a little snow mix was falling. The ground was wet and muddy. I was late getting home and nightfall was rapidly approaching. I had not taken time over the past few weeks to sharpen the saw. It needed sharpening so bad, there was no way it would cut wood without it being sharpened. I had known for days it needed to be done, but again, I put it off day after day. Suddenly, I now had an emergency.

In order to stay out of the storm, I went into a shed to sharpen the saw. The problem was that it was quite dark in the shed which made it hard to do a good job. I went to work on the saw, bending over a bit, working as fast as I could. Then the thought hit me hard.

What if the saw would not start? Sometimes it could be a bit ornery and take time, which I obviously did not have, to get it running. By the time I got the saw sharpened, my back was beginning to ache. This ache is not uncommon when I bend over in this way, but if I stop for a few minutes, stand straight and relax, it soon feels better and I can go back to work. There was, however, a major problem this time. There was no time to stand and relax. The storm was intensifying, darkness was moving quickly across the sky. Time was running out. I had to get the wood sawed. Kneeling down, I pushed the priming button four or five times, pulled the choke on, took a firm hold of the pull rope and pulled hard and fast. Nothing. Again, I pulled …nothing. Again and again, I pulled the starter rope with no success. My fears were beginning to mount. I adjusted the choke, reset the throttle and pulled. It fired, again I pulled, it fired a little more. With a hard fast pull, it started. What a relief! At last, I could saw some wood.

By this time, the shadows of darkness were settling in, the rain and snow were pounding as the force of the wind propelled them through the air. I made my way to the wood pile with the saw still running and began to saw as fast as I could. As I bent low over the logs while controlling the saw, the pain in my back increased with each cut I made. Here I was, wet and cold, darkness closing around me and my back aching with an almost unbearable pain. My back was crying out stop, give me some relief. My mind was pleading, stop, stand up straight, let your back relax, but I knew there was no time for that now. I wish I would have sharpened the saw and gotten the wood in earlier when the sun was shining. There was no excuse. I had plenty of time and was not under pressure; but all the wishes in the world would not and does not change anything.

I forced myself to continue sawing, knowing that if I wanted to keep my house warm though the storm, I had no choice. I silently prayed for strength. As always, my prayer was answered. A kind understanding loving Heavenly Father supported me as He always had so many times in the past. I then became aware of a soft, gentle whisper deep inside. It was as if I could hear my Father in Heaven saying, "O my child. When will you learn. How many opportunities must I give you or will you wait, ignore, resist and procrastinate until time runs out. The time will come when I will no longer be able to rescue you."

Will you be able to sleep when the winds of disaster blow or the winds of illness or age or loss of a loved one, disappointment or any of the other winds of life which blow from time to time. But foremost and above all, will you be able to sleep when the wind of judgment blows as you stand sometime in eternity before the judgment bar of God to be judged according to your works, thoughts and desires. Will you be at peace then or will you have procrastinated until it is too late?

This caused me to wonder if I would have developed enough faith to save me. A dream my Great-Grandfather, James Holt, had when he was about eight years old came to my mind. He said, "I dreamed that my father sent me, in company with one of my brothers, to a neighbor's place, about three miles distant, on some errand. It appeared, that in going, we had to travel through a dark and gloomy cave where there was neither light of sun, moon nor stars. It appeared that all people traveled through this gloomy cave. After we had traveled in this awful gloom for some length of time, we emerged in the light of day, and great was the contrast. Upon the left I beheld a large building, and when we came opposite this building, I saw a man coming to the door, whom I thought was the keeper. He called to me, saying, 'James Holt, you must come in here and be tried for your faith.' There were two or three steps to the building and I thought he took hold of my hand and led me up into the building, where I beheld the hook, somewhat similar to a stilyards (steelyard) suspended to a beam overhead. He said I was to be hanged upon that hook, and if I had enough faith in God, I would not fall. But if I did not have faith in God, I would fall down in that dismal 'hell,' pointing to a trap door in a floor, where there was weeping and wailing and gnashing of teeth. I looked where he had pointed and I beheld a deep, dark pit, and as far around as I could see, I beheld people in the greatest confusion; some groaning, some shouting, and all was in a great turmoil. One person stood up in their midst, saying, 'All is well with us; we need no more revelation. The canon of Scripture is full, and we will all be saved. We need not fear.' After I beheld this, the keeper took me and hung me on the hook by the back of my vest. It soon began to rip, but I began to call upon the Lord to strengthen me and increase my faith. Suddenly my vest ceased to tear, and I hung only by the seam of my collar. The keeper now took me down, saying, 'Well done, you have got just enough faith to be saved, so you can go on your way rejoicing."

While pondering on the probing question, can I sleep when the wind blows, my mind raced from thought to thought. I thought of the prophet Alma's missionary companion, Amulek. As he accompanied the prophet, he warned the Nephites not to procrastinate the day of their repentance until it is too late. In speaking to them, he said,

"For behold, this life is the time for men to prepare to meet God; yea, behold the day of this life is the day for men to perform their labors. And now, as I said unto you before, as ye have had so many witnesses, therefore, I beseech of you that ye do not procrastinate the day of your repentance until the end; for after this day of life, which is given us to prepare for eternity, behold, if we do not improve our time while in this life, then cometh the night of darkness wherein there can be no labor performed." (Alma 34:32-33).

My thoughts stirred up a memory of my grandfather, Henry Holt, who often sang the following song:

The Great Judgment Morning

> I dreamed that the great judgment morning
> Had dawned, and the trumpet had blown;
> I dreamed that the nations had gathered
> To judgment before the white throne;
> From the throne came a bright shining angel,

And he stood on the land and the sea,
And he swore with his hand raised to Heaven,
That time was no longer to be.

Refrain

And O, what a weeping and wailing,
As the lost were told of their fate;
They cried for the rocks and the mountains,
They prayed, but their prayer was too late.
The rich man was there, but his money
Had melted and vanished away;
A pauper, he stood in the judgment,
His debts were too heavy to pay;
The great man was there, but his greatness,
When death came, was left far behind!
The angel that opened the records,
Not a trace of his greatness could find.

Refrain

The widow was there with the orphans,
God heard and remembered their cries;
No sorrow in Heaven forever,
God wiped all the tears from their eyes;
The gambler was there and the drunkard,
And the man that had sold them the drink,
With the people who gave him the license,
Together in hell they did sink.

Refrain

The moral man came to the judgment,
But self righteous rags would not do;
The men who had crucified Jesus

Had passed off as moral men, too;
The soul that had put off salvation,
"Not tonight; I'll get saved by and by,
No time now to think of religion!"
At last they had found time to die.

Refrain

And O, what a weeping and wailing,
As the lost were told of their fate;
They cried for the rocks and the mountains,
They prayed, but their prayer was too late.

As these thoughts permeated my mind, I asked myself again, can I sleep when the wind blows? Will I learn and discipline myself so I will be able to sleep when the wind blows before it is too late? Whatever kinds of wind may blow, perhaps more importantly, will I have developed enough faith to save me. There are many kinds of winds that blow in this world, winds of disaster, war, loss of employment, illness, loss of relationships and loved ones, disappointment of all kinds and finally death and judgment. The Lord said, "…if ye are prepared, ye shall not fear." To be truly prepared, we must be prepared physically, mentally, emotionally, as well as spiritually.

An old gentleman, T. Taylor, used to spend a lot of time in my Dad's repair shop. As a boy, I heard a lot of good stories. One I particularly remember was about T.'s father. When T.'s father was a boy, he was sent by his father (T.'s grandfather) to gather cattle on a beautiful summer morning. As he mounted his horse, his father asked him where his raincoat was. T.'s father replied that there was not a cloud in the sky. To this, T's grandfather exclaimed, "Any damn fool can be prepared for what they know is going to happen. It takes a wise man to be prepared for the unexpected."

May I suggest to you, who read this, whoever you may be, wherever you may find yourself and in whatever circumstance, that in your moments of quiet contemplation, you ask yourself the all important question. Can I sleep when the wind of adversity and trials of this life blow upon me and even when the ultimate wind of death and judgment come, as they surely will, do I have sufficient faith and preparation that I can be at peace and as the boy in the story, sleep in peace through the midnight storms? As you honestly answer this question, if your answer is yes, then continue to move forward and hold tight to what you are doing now. If the answer is no, or even a questionable, I am not sure, may I suggest that you evaluate yourself and make the appropriate adjustments so that when the winds of life and judgment blow, you can sleep in peace.

We are always teaching something

The blazing summer sun was beating down on the floor of the high Nevada desert. The car had no air conditioning. In the 1950s, air-conditioning was far from standard equipment, in fact, most cars did not have air conditioning. The car was winding slowly along the two-lane highway, over the hills, around the sharp curves, up and down, the sound of the low roar of the engine could be heard for miles. It was a typical summer day in Nevada. The temperature was in the low hundreds. The passengers were exhausted from the heat and hours of travel. The conditions were uncomfortable and irritating to say the least. As the car made its way through the uneven terrain, old abandoned gold and silver mines were visible in abundance across the mountainside.

The passengers were hot and thirsty; perspiration flowed freely. The canvas water bag hanging on the side of the car provided some relief as it was passed from passenger to passenger for a small drink of water. Cautions were given not to drink too much, because it had to last until we reached the next town which was still many miles away. After everyone had a drink, the water bag was placed back outside the car with the rope handle secured over the mirror. The wind blowing past the bag would help to keep the water cool, but I assure you it was a long way from being ice water.

This was the scene as my parents, my Grandfather Holt, who was well up in his 80s, and I returned from my uncle and aunt's house in Fallon, Nevada to our home in Parowan, Utah. I was almost 5 years old and I learned a great lesson that day. This lesson has stayed with me my entire life. Lessons that are well taught and learned always do stay with us. My mother and dad were both complaining about the heat and how miserable, hot and tired they were. At the same time, Grandpa Holt and I sat in the backseat just as hot, just as tired and just as miserable, but there was a wonderful difference. Grandpa was joyful, singing song after song, he was relaxed and happy as the car rolled along mile after mile. What a great lesson Grandpa taught that day without saying a word . He did not allow the environment to control his attitude and his happiness. William James said that the greatest discovery of the 19th century is that a man can change his environment by changing his attitude

Another great lesson came a few years later when I was a young teenager. My dad and I would often take cattle to the livestock auction in Cedar City, Utah. A lot of the time we would not have a full load and if any of the other farmers had an animal to sell, we would haul it to the auction for them. At that time the Church of Jesus Christ of Latter-day Saints had welfare projects of some kind in most of the stakes. In the Church of Jesus Christ of Latter-Day Saints, the term stake refers to a geographical area which contains several smaller congregational units referred to as wards. Each stake generally consists of somewhere around five or six wards. Some stakes would have honey bees and provide honey for a project. Another stake might raise beef cattle while another stake would raise some kind of vegetables and so on. These items would be sent to a central location known as the Bishops Storehouse for distribution to those in need, members and non-members alike. Our stake project was raising dairy calves to be sent to a dairy in California.

There was a man who was a prominent member of the community and an active church member. He had held and continued to hold high church positions in our local area. He was in charge of and managed the church farm. He called my dad and told him he had a heifer he needed to send to the auction. We were going that next Saturday and had room, so dad said he would be glad to take it. Early Saturday morning, dad and I loaded our cattle and headed off to the church farm. This man was there to meet us. We backed up to the loading chute and loaded the heifer. As the heifer came into the truck, dad noticed a hole in her right side. Dad made a comment about the hole to which the man said that she is a bloater and that is why he was selling her. A bloater is a cow that has a digestive problem which causes it to bloat when it eats. Bloating is a potential killer. Death is inevitable for an animal who has a chronic bloating problem. When a cow is on the verge of dying from bloat, there is a temporary solution. By taking a knife and puncturing into the stomach at a certain place on the right side of the cow the pressure is relieved. This, however, is not a permanent cure. The cow will continue to bloat again and again until it finally dies. Dad said to this man that she wouldn't bring much money. To this, the man replied that he would take care of that. He took a pitchfork, reached into the corral, got a forkful of wet straw manure, and spread it over the hole on the heifer's side, saying that no one will know. With this, dad and I went off to the auction. As I recall, the heifer brought a good price and like the man had said no one knew. Really! Really! I knew, dad knew, he knew, God knew, and the person that bought the heifer knew, because a cover-up of that kind does not last long. Of course, everyone that the buyer told, as he no doubt did, would know.

I was taught a great lesson that day. My mind ran wild. As a young boy, I had difficulty understanding what I had just witnessed. Many questions ran through my mind. How could a man do such a dishonest thing? How could a man representing the church do something that he knows would surely reflect negatively on the church? How could a highly respected man, one holding high positions in the church and community, do such a thing? As a young boy, I tried to sort this issue out in my mind. I knew what he did was wrong. It was dishonest, yet he was a respected man in the community and the church. I saw him in church each Sunday exercising the priesthood, leading and teaching others about right and wrong and about the ways of righteousness. This bothered me for years. It certainly had a great impact on my mind. Here it is over 50 years later and I still remember it as if it were yesterday.

It took me many years to work through this in my mind. I must say that I did learn a lot from this experience. Over the years, I have come to realize that the church is not the people in the church. Regardless of what people in the church may do, it does not change the truth of the church. I have also learned that the church is not the gospel. The gospel of Jesus Christ, as restored in these the latter days through the prophet Joseph Smith, has the authority and power to administer the ordinances of salvation. Even though the saving ordinances of salvation are administered through the church, the church and the gospel are not one in the same. The gospel is true, correct and perfect, but it is administered through imperfect men here on the earth. It is easy to equate the actions of imperfect men with the church and the gospel. This is a grievous mistake which should never be made. Each of us must guard against making this mistake in our own life and never allow ourselves to get caught in this most destructive trap. I also learned that no matter what position a person holds in church, community, business, or any other place, that in and of itself means nothing as to the integrity and character of the individual holding the position.

Another experience of a different type occurred when I was 16 years old. In our church there was a youth program at that time, known as the Mutual Improvement Association (MIA). As part of the MIA program, the youth would put on what was called a roadshow. A roadshow is a play that the youth group from each ward puts on for each ward in the stake. Each ward would rotate throughout the stake, sharing their play with the other wards.

It was roadshow time and I was at MIA. There were a number of us boys in the foyer of the church just messing around, doing whatever it is 16-year-old boys do. I knew it was time to prepare for the roadshow. I was planning to be in it, as I enjoyed being in plays and doing that kind of thing. About that time the lady in our ward who had been called to be in charge of the roadshow came into the foyer. As she entered, she announced in a rather loud and a very demanding voice something to the effect of-you boys get in here, referring to the cultural hall, right now. You have to be in this play. I am not sure if it was her attitude, tone of voice, or the demanding or most likely, a combination of all three, whatever the case, it hit me wrong, I looked at her and said I don't have to do a damn thing. Turning, I left the church, went downtown for a while, then went home. As an adult now I can only imagine the conversations that went on behind the scenes regarding me. What I do know is my mother begged, pleaded and cried. The Bishop, who is the ecclesiastical leader, came to my house and talked with me. In spite of all that was done, there was no changing my mind. I absolutely refused to be in that play. Ironically, about three months later there was a stake play which I willingly volunteered to be in, and as always, I had a great time.

Once again, there were great lessons taught by this lady that night. Perhaps one of the most valuable lessons I learned was as we interact with others, we have an impact that may stick for a long time. Here I am 54 years later still remembering and still feeling, to some extent, the effects of that experience. I want to make it very clear. I hold absolutely no animosity or ill feelings toward her in any way. As an adult, I understand she was no doubt under pressure. She was probably frustrated and worried. She may not have been feeling very well. There may have been things going on in her personal life, which had nothing to do with the play or those of us who she needed to be in it. Maybe she just did not understand, or perhaps she felt some kind of power in being an adult and felt she had some kind of right to exercise control over us. Whatever the case may have been, it did not work. In fact, it left long lasting deep wounds that were totally unnecessary.

The Lord has taught us how to deal effectively with others. If we would only listen, learn and apply. Do unto others as you would have others do unto you. Paraphrasing-treat others the way you want to be treated. How simple, but yet how seldom done. Another lesson I learned from this experience that has served me well through my life is to never, never try to force others to do anything. Force is contrary to the laws of heaven, and will never bring positive results. It is important to understand that everything we do we choose to do. We cannot make or force anyone to do anything until they choose to do it.

On the other side of the coin is a story a man told of an experience he had as a young boy lying all alone in a hospital bed on Thanksgiving day waiting for a surgery. His mother was very poor and did not have enough money to make the trip to the hospital. He said as the day slowly progressed, a great feeling of despair gripped his entire body. He was so alone. He thought of his mother home alone with little to eat and not enough money to do anything about it. Pulling the covers over his head so as to not be seen, he began to sob. Soon his entire body was racked with pain and agony as his uncontrollable sobbing went through his entire being.

A student nurse passing by heard his sobbing and going to his bed side, pulled the covers back and gently wiped the tears from his face. She explained to this little boy that she was all alone for Thanksgiving and asked if he would be so kind as to have dinner with her. After they had eaten dinner, she continued to talk with him. Her shift had ended about 5 o'clock, but she continued to talk and play games with him. She stayed with him, giving him comfort and support until after 11 o'clock. What a powerful impact. What lessons were taught as a result of her implementing one simple principle—do unto others as you would have others do unto you.

Jim Fay, the author of Discipline with Love and Logic, tells a story of a little girl who came home from school and excitedly exclaimed to her father that she got 100% on her spelling test that day. Dad, who was sitting in his easy chair reading his newspaper, didn't even look up and said that's good. A few days later, the little girl ran into the house exclaiming with excitement that she passed her seven times tables off today. Again, Dad responded with no emotion, without looking up - that's good. Over time this type of thing continue to occur until one day the girl came into the house and announced dad, the kids would not play with me today. Dad quickly laid his paper down, looked his daughter in the eye and with great emotion, asked her what she meant that the kids would not play with her. The girl responded that she wanted to play on the swings and the teeter totter and they wanted to play ball. Dad quickly explained that if you want to have friends, you can't just do what you want. You have to do what they want to do.

Time passed and this interaction between dad and daughter had been long forgotten, but the lesson taught had not. One night when the daughter was about 15 years old, she came home late and had obviously been drinking. Dad was appalled. He asked her what she was thinking and why would she do that because she knew better. Dad could not understand why his daughter would do such a thing. Then his daughter replied the simple, but powerful truth as she said that her friends were drinking. The lesson which she had been taught and learned so well many years earlier was now in effect. Dad, without realizing it, had taught her that friends are very important; more so than grades, more than learning and perhaps more important than anything, even family. The great impact of this lesson had been planted deeply within this young girl. The lesson was that if you want to have friends, you can't just do what you want to do, you have to do what they want to do.

Once again, remember, we are always teaching something. It would do well for each of us to pay close attention and give serious thought to what we are teaching, even when we think we are not teaching. We cannot **not** make a choice, because if we choose not to choose, that very act is an act of choice. In the same way, we cannot **not** teach, even if we attempt not to teach, we are, in fact, teaching. Every interaction we have will have an impact of some type, no matter how small. Something will be taught, lessons will be learned and feelings will be touched. Even though it may be minute, lives will be altered either for good or bad, right or wrong. It behooves each of us to be aware and ask ourselves continually, what am I teaching?

Eagle or Chicken

An old farmer was out working on his farm when he noticed a large egg lying on the ground. He picked up the egg and wondered what kind it was. As he looked at the egg, he thought about a hen back in the barnyard setting on some eggs. He had a great idea, "I will put the egg with the others and let the hen hatch it and then I will know what it is." That is exactly what he did. After a few days had passed, the egg hatched and low and behold, it was a baby eagle. The farmer thought that was cool, so he just left the eagle with the baby chicks and they grew up together. As the days went by, they ran around the barnyard scratching and pecking in the dirt. The eagle was contented and happy. He was just one of the chickens. Now, he did not look like a chicken, as he was much bigger and had long beautiful wings and gorgeous feathers. The eagle had always been with the chickens, had learned to act like the chickens, so he figured he was just one of the chickens, even though he looked nothing like them.

One day, a naturalist was passing by the farm. (A naturalist is a person who studies plants and animals in the natural environment.) The naturalist saw a beautiful eagle out in the barnyard running around with the chickens. He quickly stopped his car to get a better look. He could not believe his eyes. Sure enough, it was an eagle out there scratching and pecking in the dirt, acting just like the chickens. The naturalist walked over to the farmhouse and knocked on the door.

When the farmer came to the door, the naturalist said to the farmer, "Do you know you have an eagle out there with your chickens?"

The farmer replied, "No, there are only chickens in the barnyard."

The naturalist said, "Come with me and I will show you."

They walked to the barnyard together. The naturalist pointed to the eagle and said, "That is an eagle."

The farmer said, "No, that is just one of the chickens."

The naturalist said, "No, that is an eagle. I will show you."

The naturalist caught the eagle, set him on the fence, held his head up so he could look into the sky and said, "You are an eagle… Fly!"

The eagle looked up, then looked down into the barnyard and saw his chicken friends. He jumped off the fence and started scratching and pecking with the chickens.

The farmer said to the naturalist, "See, I told you. That is a chicken."

The naturalist said, "No, that is an eagle. I will come back tomorrow and show you."

The following day the naturalist returned to the farm. He caught the eagle, put him on top of the barn, held his head up high so he could look at the sky and said, "You are an eagle…Fly!"

The eagle looked up then he looked down and saw all his chicken friends scratching and pecking on the ground. He jumped down and quickly joined them doing what chickens do best, just running around scratching and pecking in the dirt.

At that, the farmer again replied, "See, I told you… just a chicken."

The naturalist again insisted that it was an eagle. He said, "I will come back tomorrow and show you."

The naturalist returned the next day, caught the eagle and took him a long way from the barnyard. He put him on a high ledge, held his head up so he could look into the sky and said, "You are an eagle…Fly!" The eagle looked up; then he looked down and could see nothing but space and countryside. He looked up into the sky, spread his enormous powerful wings and jumped from the ledge. His wings caught the air and began to do what they were created to do, lifting the beautiful marvelous bird higher and higher. With power and grace, he soared away until he was out of sight. The naturalist turned to the farmer and said, "Now that is an eagle."

When the eagle was in the barnyard, he was satisfied with just being a chicken. That is all he knew. Because the chickens spent their life looking at the ground so they could scratch and peck in the dirt, he did the same thing. The problem is, it is hard to look up when your focus is down.

Ask yourself these questions:

Am I a chicken or an eagle?
Do I spend my time in the barnyard scratching and
pecking with the chickens?
Do I spend my time focusing on the ground or do I look up?

How much time do I spend looking at the ground with the chickens and how much time do I spend looking up with the eagles?

It is very important to know who we really are. We read in the scriptures in Moses about his experience when he saw God Three times God referred to Moses as His son. God wanted Moses to know that he was a son of God. He wanted Moses to understand that he (Moses) was an eagle. After God left Moses, Satan appeared. Satan addressed Moses by saying, "Moses, son of man..." (Moses 1:12) Satan wanted Moses to think he was just an ordinary man. He wanted him to believe he was nothing more than a chicken. When God the Father and His son, Jesus Christ, appeared to Joseph Smith, God spoke to Joseph, calling him by name. God wanted Joseph to know that he (God) knew him. Yes! God knew Joseph by name. God wanted Joseph to understand that he was an eagle even though he was living in the barnyard (on earth) with the chickens.

In the Book of Abraham, we read about a great meeting held in the pre-existence. All the spirits were gathered there as God explained his plan for us, so we could have the opportunity to become like him. God stated that among these spirits were many of the noble and great ones. God exclaimed, "These I will make my rulers." (Abraham 3:23) In other words, they are eagles. They will go to the earth into the barnyard with all the chickens, but if they will look up and focus on Heavenly Father and spread their wings, with His help, they will fly. Heavenly Father will teach them to soar with power and beauty high into the heavens even to eternal life and exaltation. You are one of these. You are one of the noble and great ones spoken of in the scriptures. You are one of the ones of which God said, "These I will make my rulers."

You are here on earth, as it were, in the barnyard with the chickens and that is where Satan wants you to stay. Satan wants you to believe you are just a chicken. He wants you to see yourself as a chicken. He wants you to spend your life just pecking and scratching around with all the other chickens. You need to always remember you are not a chicken, you are an eagle. You came to this earth for a special purpose. You came to the earth to soar high and be with the eagles. With the help of our Father in Heaven, that is exactly what you will do. As you experience life in your own unique beautiful way, always remember who you are. You are a child of God and were born to be an eagle. When you have temptations, as you will, and must make choices, remember, remember who you are. Always ask yourself if this choice will lift me into the heavens with the eagles or will it keep me on the ground in the barnyard with the chickens? Remember, it is hard to look up when your focus is on the ground. Keep your focus high, looking into the sky. Spread your wings and soar. Fill the measure of your creation and become the eagle you were born to be.

What if

If, if, if, if only, if not, if you would have, if I could have, if I hadn't of, if you hadn't of, if, if, if. The world is full of ifs. We hear ifs of all kinds, from almost everyone and even if we don't hear them spoken, they are most likely there in the minds of all people at one time or another. As I contemplate the ifs of my own life and the ifs I have heard from others, my thoughts turn to a story I call the maybe, maybe not story.

It seems that many years ago there was a poor peasant named Hans who lived in a far-off country. Hans and his family's survival was dependent on the food they were able to raise on the few acres of land they farmed. He worked diligently in the spring, preparing and planting the ground. He watched, watered, weeded, and carefully cared for the crops through the summer. In the fall, he would carefully harvest and store the food he had raised. Without the long hard hours of preparation, he and his family would surely starve to death, as they had no other means of obtaining food for the winter.

Hans often thanked his Father in Heaven for the blessings he had. He had been blessed with land on which to raise food and the means to do so. He had been blessed with a son to help him with the long hours of hard labor. He had been blessed with a wonderful ox with which to work the land. Though he had some underlying concern about the crops he planted each year, he had great faith and felt a certain sense of security as year after year things had gone rather well and he had always been able to raise sufficient food for his family's need.

One day in the early spring, Hans arose from bed looking forward to the day. It was time to begin his spring work in preparation for planting. As he went about his usual morning activities of preparing for the day, he felt good inside. It was a beautiful spring day. Hans glanced out of the window as he was finishing breakfast; just in time to catch a glimpse of the sun peeking over the horizon. There was not a cloud in the sky. Upon leaving his house to go to the barnyard, he became aware of a peace and serenity that seemed to flow endlessly across the valley. Hans was filled with anticipation as he contemplated hooking his ox to the plow and going to work on such a gorgeous day.

As Hans went out to work his land that day in preparation for planting, what he saw when he looked over the fence caused a surge of panic and fear to radiate through his mind and body like a bolt of lightning. He could not believe his eyes. There, on the other side of the fence, lay his ox, stiff and cold. His ox had died. Without his ox he would be unable to work the ground and without proper preparation, the seeds would not grow and produce the needed food for the winter. Thoughts of uncertainty flooded his mind and he wondered what to do. As he thought about his situation and struggling to come up with a solution, a wonderful thought crossed his mind. He would go to the wise man of the country and ask him what he should do. Hans quickly made the necessary preparations and set off to see the wise man. This wise man was noted for his wisdom, knowledge and understanding. He was noted for having answers and being able to find solutions for problems. Hans felt certain once he was able to talk to the wise man, his problem would be solved.

After traveling for many hours, he finally reached the home of the wise man. Upon entering and being granted audience with this wise man of the country, he told the wise man that the worst thing that could possibly have happened, did happen to him. Hans related his situation, explaining that his ox had died and without his ox to work the ground, his family would surely be doomed to starvation in the coming winter. The wise man listened intently. He looked directly into Hans's eyes with the piercing eyes of wisdom that seemed to penetrate deep into Han's very soul and gently said, "Maybe, maybe not." With the maybe, maybe not answer from the wise man, Hans left the wise man's home. The wise man's statement, maybe, maybe not, weighed heavily on Hans's mind as he took his journey home. With only the maybe, maybe not explanation from the wise man, Hans was feeling very disappointed. He began to wonder how the wise man could be so dumb.

Upon arriving home, Hans told his friends and family of his experience. Hans was very upset. He had taken his time and energy to go visit the wise man in order to get help with the worst thing that could ever have happened to him and all the wise man had to say was maybe, maybe not. Exhausted, frustrated and still worried, Hans went to bed and after some time, sleep overtook him. The next morning Hans awakened, arose from his bed and went to the door, with the intent of breathing in some cool fresh air of the glorious spring morning. As he opened the door, he was astonished at what he beheld. There, caught in the fence, was a beautiful, muscular, healthy looking horse. Hans quickly approached the horse and as he did, he was pleasantly surprised and excited to find the horse was gentle and obviously well-trained. Hans carefully freed the horse from the fence and led him to the barnyard. Suddenly, Hans had a great idea. Maybe I can use this horse to plow and work the ground. Hans could hardly wait to get the horse in a harness and hook him to the plow. Hans was so hopeful and excited. Finally, everything was in place. The horse was hooked to the plow and then came the true test. Thoughts flashed wildly through his mind. Is this going to work? Will the horse know how to pull a plow? With these and many other questions flooding Hans' mind, he took the reins, gave them a gentle shake and yelled giddy-up. Hans was extremely joyful and excited to find that the horse was well-trained and responded properly. Hans went through his field plowing row after row. Hans thought that this was a great blessing and he must go and tell the wise man.

Hans quickly took his journey once again to see the wise man. Upon reaching the wise man's home, Hans was once again brought before the wise man. Hans excitedly exclaimed, "You were exactly right! My ox dying was not the worst thing that could've possibly happened to me, in fact, it was the best thing that could've happened." Hans explained to the wise man that he had found a horse and was now able to plow much faster. He could now plow and work his ground four or five times faster than he could with his ox. Therefore, he would be able not only to raise enough food for his family, but would be able to raise extra so he would have things to sell which would be a great blessing to him for the upcoming winter. Having my ox die was really the best thing that could've happened to me. Once again, the wise man, with thoughtful, penetrating eyes, looked into Hans's face and gently said, " Maybe, maybe not."

With this, Hans once again left the wise man's home pondering the statement, maybe, maybe not. Hans was beginning to think perhaps the wise man was not so wise. The very best thing that could've happened to me has happened and again all the wise man had to say is maybe, maybe not. Hans returned home and related his experience to his family and friends telling them of the wise man and expressing his doubts about the wise man's wisdom. Hans told his family and friends the best thing that could possibly have happened to him happened and all the wise man could say was maybe, maybe not.

The next day the farmer and his son were working in the field. His son was plowing with the horse making really good progress. It was a typical spring day . Hans noticed a few dark clouds appear on the far distant western horizon. This was of little concern to Hans, as this was a very common scene that Hans had observed many times. As Han's son slowly made his way up and down the field, plowing row after row, the wind began to blow. At first it was a nice, peaceful breeze, but it quickly began to intensify. The black clouds were no longer so distant, in fact, they were rolling across the sky as though they were great ocean waves, one after another, preparing to heave themselves beyond their bounds. The sky was quickly becoming black and foreboding. Hans knew a storm was imminent. He beckoned to his son to stop plowing, take the horse and head for shelter.

As Hans' son was trying to unhook the horse from the plow; it happened. A blinding bolt of lightning flashed across the sky and found its way to its final destination at the end of the field with a great explosion of an ear-deafening clap of thunder. The horse jumped and bolted forward with great strength and in doing so, Hans' son's leg, having been caught in the plow, was badly broken. Shock surged through Hans' body and settled as a knot deep in the pit of his stomach. Hans realized his son would not be able to work and help him for the entire summer. He would not be able to accomplish all his work because he could not do it alone. Once again, Hans thought the wise man was correct. Having his ox die and finding the horse was not the best thing that could've happened to him; it really was the worst. Now his son has a broken leg, will be unable to work and help him for a long time and they will surely starve this winter.

With this dilemma weighing heavily on Hans' mind, he again returned to see the wise man. As he sat in audience with the wise man, he exclaimed, "You were correct. Finding the horse was not the best thing that could've happened to me, in fact, it was the worst. Now my son has a broken leg and is unable to help me with the work. I'm right back where I was in the beginning, as I will not be able to raise sufficient food for my family and we will surely starve this winter." Hans was again surprised and filled with wonderment to hear the wise man exclaim, "Maybe, maybe not." Hans left and returned home, continuing to feel somewhat distraught concerning the wise man. He wondered why the only thing the wise man could say was maybe, maybe not.

Hans talked with his friends and family and continued to express his frustration and exclaimed that he did not understand how the wise men could be regarded as a wise man. All he ever says, no matter what happens to me, is maybe, maybe not. The following day war broke out in the country and all the young men were called to war except Hans's son, who could not go because of his broken leg. The young men of the country went to battle and all were killed. Had Hans' son been with them, he would've lost his life; therefore, having a broken leg was not really the worst thing that could have happened to Hans. In fact, it was really the best or was it? Maybe, maybe not.

With all the challenges and various experiences life has to offer, we have the opportunity to make choices and decisions. Sometimes those choices and decisions bring about good and positive results. Other times they bring negative and sometimes painful and undesirable results. It is easy to look back and say if only I had done it differently; if this or that had not have happened; if only I had chosen a different route. When we get caught up in the ifs and the if onlys, we tend to think things would have been better had we chosen a different route; if so-and-so had not have done what they did or if things had not happened the way they happened.

In reality, as the story of Hans and his visit to the wise man points out, all we know for sure is maybe, maybe not. There is no way of knowing absolutely what the difference would be had we made a different choice, had things have gone differently, had we not had the flood, or the tornado, or the fire, or the accident, or the illness. It's easy to believe that if only things had been different; if only I had made a different choice. If things had happened differently, then the results would be different. If only things had not happened as they did, then I would be better off and my life would be better…. I would be happier, or more successful. It is true that had things been different than they were, then things would be different than they are, but there is no way of knowing for sure that the difference would be positive, would have been better for us, or that we would be happier or better off in any way. We are, therefore, left with the wise man's counsel; maybe, maybe not. It is true that all choices and decisions have a consequence, and in many cases the consequence of a different choice and decision would have produced a better outcome. However, there is also a chance that that different choice and decision would have produced a less desirable consequence and may have inhibited our growth and development.

Concerning things of the environment over which we have no choice such as the ox dying, the horse bolting and breaking the son's leg, death, illness, injury or the loss of a home to the fire, tornado, or flood. Of course, the list goes on and on. Had these things not occurred, circumstances would most certainly have been different. However, there is no way of knowing that the difference is one we would prefer rather than the one we now experience. Once again, we are left with the wise man's counsel of maybe, maybe not.

One thing that is certain, whatever has occurred in our life, whatever we have experienced, either good or bad, joyful or painful, is water under the bridge. It cannot be changed, it is written in the history of our life. The choices and decisions we have made which led to the consequences we experience as a result of those choices and decisions is also water under the bridge and cannot be changed. To waste time and energy caught in the if's and what if's is like standing on a bridge, gazing down into a river trying to get the water that went under that bridge somewhere in the past five, 10, or even 30 or more years ago to come back and pass under the bridge again, so that in some way we can alter its flow. Of course, that is impossible. Water that has gone under the bridge is gone forever. Experiences and consequences of the past are also gone forever. They cannot be changed. We can spend our time wallowing in self-pity, sadness, feeling miserable, worrying about what if this or what if that, if only, or we can accept the fact that yes, things would be different but would it really be better.... maybe, maybe not. We can be wise and learn to accept things as they are and use those experiences to our benefit. We can use the consequences of our choices and decisions to learn, to improve, to overcome, to gain greater strength and faith and to direct our life in a more positive direction.

Many times I have heard people say, if only I had my life to live over knowing what I know now, inferring that if they had the opportunity to live their life over knowing what they know now, they would do some things differently. The ironic thing is that is exactly what each of us have, regardless of where we find ourselves at the present time. We have our life to live from this point on knowing what we now know.

There is great danger in spending too much time looking behind. There is a great message in the experience of Lot and his wife as they left the city of Sodom. (Genesis 19:26) They were instructed not to look back; however, Lot's wife apparently found it difficult to leave the past behind, paused to look back and was turned into a pillar of salt. I have heard it said that God put eyes in front of us so we would not have to look behind. May we all be wise and use the past as learning experiences, then move forward in faith with our eyes fixed firmly on our goal. May we use the water that has gone under our personal bridge and experiences associated with it, to make better choices, decisions and improve our life from this point on throughout the rest of our life. Remember where we come from and where we have been is no longer important. The important thing is where we are headed today and where we end.

Hauling Wood

It was very early one morning, as I sat pondering life, when my thoughts turned toward my own mortality. Personal questions began to run through my mind. What have I done with my life? How important are the things I have done? What value to me or others are the things I have done? Then the even more important questions began to come. What am I going to do with the rest of my life? What does my Father in Heaven want me to do with the rest of my life? What am I expected to accomplish before I leave this earth and move on into eternity? As these and other related thoughts floated across my mind, I felt a strong need to kneel before my Heavenly Father and talk with him. I knelt down and began to pray, seeking to know what my Heavenly Father would have me do with the rest of my life. As I prayed, a profound thought came to my mind in the form of the following story:

There was a man who awakened early one sunny crisp fall day. Quickly he ate his breakfast, packed a lunch and went into the barnyard. He hitched his team of horses to a wagon. He picked up his ax, chain, bar and wedges and put them into the wagon, climbed on and was ready to go. Taking the reins in both hands, giving them a shake as he spoke to his team, he was off. After traveling a couple of hours, he arrived at his destination deep in the woods. The trees were plentiful, it was such a beautiful day and the warm sun rays soothed his body. There was a hint of fall in the cool, refreshing breeze. The day was perfect for hauling wood.

As he climbed off his wagon, his thoughts turned to the things of eternity. He thought of Heavenly Father and our Savior, Jesus Christ. He thought of his faith and his testimony. He knew without a doubt there is a Father in Heaven who has all power. The man thought, Heavenly Father can do anything, he knows and loves me; after all, I am his son. I know I am a good man, I do my best to keep Heavenly Father's commandments. I know my Father in Heaven has promised to help me if I will but ask. With these thoughts running through his mind and feeling tired after a long wagon ride, he knelt beside his wagon and offered a prayer. He explained to his Father in Heaven that he was very tired with not getting much sleep the night before and traveling so far on the wagon. He discussed his problems and explained how badly he needed a load of wood. With great faith and sincere desire, he fervently asked his Heavenly Father for the wagon load of wood he needed so badly. Upon concluding his prayer and feeling great faith, he climbed under the wagon and fell into a deep, peaceful sleep.

After a few hours of good sleep, he awakened and crawled out from under the wagon. Looking around, he was astonished and dismayed to find nothing had changed. There was no wood on the wagon. There were no trees cut down. As far as he could see, Heavenly Father had done absolutely nothing.

Is this story absurd? Is it ridiculous? No rational thinking human being would expect or even think that Heavenly Father would load the wagon for the man while he slept. Yet often in our own life and in other ways, that is exactly what we do. We may not climb under a wagon and sleep, waiting for Heavenly Father to load the wood while we do nothing. We go about our everyday business waiting for something to happen, letting precious time slip away, expecting Heavenly Father to take care of us, give us some revelation or at least inspiration when we do nothing but ask. If we want results, we must do something.

Heavenly Father has given us many wonderful talents and abilities. He has given us a mind, body and intelligence and the Light of Christ to guide us. He expects us to be proactive and do all we can. He expects us to use our gifts, talents and intelligence; in short, he expects us to choose a tree, pick up the ax and start swinging. When we do that he will guide the blade and he will strengthen our arms and back. He will protect, support, and guide us in every possible way. When we exercise our faith through action and use the abilities Heavenly Father has given us, he will, in his loving wisdom, fill in where we fall short. He will see to it that we reach our goals and objectives as long as they are in keeping with His mind and will. If by chance, due to our poor judgment, we choose a goal which takes us in the wrong direction, He will gently correct our course to align with His will, if we are willing to listen to and trust in Him. The important thing to remember is that Heavenly Father cannot correct our course until we take a step. He cannot strengthen our arms and back until we swing the ax. We must get out from under the wagon, pick up the ax, walk to the tree and go to work, if we expect Heavenly Father to help us.

We find a great example of this principle in the Bible. In 1st Samuel chapter 17, we read about the Israelites at a time when they were at war with the Philistines. The Israelite army was in trouble. They were paralyzed with fear because of the extraordinary weapon the Philistines possessed. This weapon was a great giant named Goliath. Goliath was about nine feet tall and weighed several hundred pounds. With his great size, extraordinary strength and full body armor, he was a fierce sight to behold. As he walked out on the hillside across the valley from the Israelite armies, they trembled with fear. Day after day, Goliath would stand on the side of the hill and shout challenges to the Israelites. The challenge was simple. Send someone out to fight me in a fight to the death. If I win, you surrender to us. If your man wins, we surrender to you and the war will be over. This daily challenge had been going on for some time when a young shepherd boy named David appeared on the scene.

David was the youngest of several brothers. They were sons of an ordinary Israelite man named Jesse. There was nothing that appeared to be very special about David. However, a few years before this, the prophet Samuel was commanded by Heavenly

Father to anoint a future king. After searching and being led by the Spirit, he was directed to Jesse's home, where he interviewed all of Jesse's sons, except David. David, being the youngest son, was tending his father's sheep and was not available. Upon learning that Jesse had one more son, Samuel asked for David to be brought to him. After sending for David and meeting him, the Lord told Samuel that this young inconsequential boy was to be the next king of Israel. Samuel anointed him to be such and things went on pretty much as normal, with David continuing to care for his father's sheep.

When David arrived at the battle front to bring food to his older brothers, he was astonished to hear Goliath's threats and challenges toward the Israelites and their Heavenly Father. David could not understand why all the soldiers refused to accept Goliath's challenge. David said that we are Heavenly Father's people, Heavenly Father is with us, so why won't someone go out and fight Goliath, but everyone was afraid. Goliath was so big, so loud, so frightening; after all, he was a giant. This bothered David and he continued to ask the question, why doesn't someone accept Goliath's challenge? When word reached King Saul about all that David had to say, the king called David to come and talk with him. David asked King Saul the same question. Why don't we do something about this Goliath? King Saul's response was that everyone is afraid. The conversation continued between David and King Saul. David insisted that we are Heavenly Father's people and Heavenly Father has promised to be with us; therefore, Heavenly Father will help us but someone has to go and fight. By this time it must have become evident to David that no one was going to go up against Goliath; therefore, he volunteered. King Saul was reluctant at first to let such a young and totally inexperienced boy go out to fight this giant knowing the entire fate of Israel would be held in those two small hands. Whatever the reason, King Saul finally agreed to allow David to go into the battlefield against Goliath.

King Saul wanted to give David all the help he could. He offered David his personal sword and armor, but David refused. David told

Saul that he was really just a shepherd boy and was not a warrior. David knew he had to approach this great challenge being just who and what he was, trusting Heavenly Father to strengthen and support him. Goliath was contacted, the challenge was accepted and the time for the battle was set.

As the time for the contest approached, David, with faith, prepared himself through prayer, asking Heavenly Father to strengthen and support him. He took his slingshot, which was the only weapon he knew how to use, went down to a nearby creek bed and found some nice, smooth stones which were just right for his slingshot. With this preparation being made, he was ready to meet Goliath.

As David left the ranks of the Israelite army and walked across the valley toward the Philistines, Goliath could not believe his eyes. He began to laugh and jeer and was almost in a state of shock. He was highly insulted thinking that the Israelites would send such a little boy, with no training, to fight a mighty giant warrior. He must have been thinking, how easy can this be? The thing Goliath did not understand was the power and workings of Heavenly Father. David continued to approach Goliath until he reached a point which was a good throwing distance for David's slingshot. Goliath was still jeering and laughing as David stopped and placed a rock in the pouch of his slingshot. Goliath must have wondered what was going on as David began to swing his slingshot around and around his head. Then, with precision, as David had done so many times to protect his father's sheep from wild animals, the rock was released. The rock travelled fast, its path was straight and sure, as it made contact on a vital area of Goliath's head. The giant fell with a great thud. The great giant warrior lay dead on the ground. He had been slain at the hands of the little Israelite boy with a slingshot.

In our modern society there seems to be an overwhelming attitude, which I refer to as entitlement mentality. Many people seem to feel someone should take care of them. The government should fix it for me. The church should fix it for me. The neighbor should fix it for me. The insurance company should fix it for me.

This mentality goes on and on. After all, no matter what happens, it must be the fault of someone or something other than me; therefore, someone other than myself should fix it for me. Even if it is my fault, someone should come to my rescue. Due to the strength of society's influence on us, it is very easy to get caught up in this entitlement thinking. When that happens, this attitude not only affects our everyday relationships with each other, but can very easily get mentally transferred into our relationship with our Father in Heaven.

We pray for those who are sick and unable to meet their needs. We pray for those who are inactive in the church and have lost their way. We are quick to let them know we are praying for them. We make statements such as, we are praying for you, you are in our prayers or we want you to know we love you. We ask members to pray for brother and sister so and so, sometimes we even fast for brother and sister so and so, then rather than pick up our ax and go to work, rendering help and service, we crawl under our wagon and go to sleep, expecting the Lord to do the work or, in another words, load the wagon for us. We pray both individually and collectively for our friends and neighbors to accept the gospel and to join the church. We talk of our love for them, and how the gospel would bring blessings into their life. We then go merrily on our way and allow our time to be used with inconsequential everyday activities. If we are not careful, we may find ourselves spending our life under the wagon. Believing we are exercising faith, we wait for Heavenly Father to let us know what to do. We wait for the government, the neighbor, the community, the family, or anyone or anything that may come along, to load the wagon for us as our whole life slips away.

On this same topic in the Bible, James wrote these words in Chapter 2, verses 14 – 20:

> 14 What doth it profit, my brethren, though a man say he hath faith, and have not works? can faith save him?

15 If a brother or sister be naked, and destitute of daily food,

16 And one of you say unto them, Depart in peace, be ye warmed and filled; notwithstanding ye give them not those things which are needful to the body; what doth it profit?

17 Even so faith, if it hath not works, is dead, being alone.

18 Yea, a man may say, Thou hast faith, and I have works: shew me thy faith without thy works, and I will shew thee my faith by my works.

19 Thou believest that there is one God; thou doest well: the devils also believe, and tremble.

20 But wilt thou know, O vain man, that faith without works is dead?

David appeared to have great faith, as demonstrated by his attitude and comments among the Israelite soldiers and in his conversation with King Saul; his fervor in expressing the fact that they were Heavenly Father's people and Heavenly Father would help them; along with his insistence that someone should come forth to fight Goliath and finally, his willingness to do it himself. In spite of all the expression and appearance of faith, it was not until he took action by taking his slingshot, going to the river bed, picking up rocks, walking up the hill toward Goliath, putting the rock in the slingshot pouch, swinging the sling around his head and releasing the rock that positive results occurred. Once David took action, Heavenly Father helped him every step of the way. David was given strength, guidance and support until the final objective was achieved.

President Gordon B. Hinckley said, "let us get our instruments tightly strung and our melodies sweetly sung. Let us not die with our music still in us." Getting our instruments tightly strung and our melodies sweetly sung denotes action. We must pick up our ax and start swinging. If we do this, exercising faith, courage and striving to live a righteous life, we will not die with our music still in us. We will, in fact, make a difference to someone, somewhere, and most certainly to ourselves.

Fairness, Favoritism and Equal Treatment

George's alarm clock began to ring. It was time to rise and shine. That was not a problem for George since he loved his work as a teacher. He looked forward each day with excitement and enthusiasm at the prospects of standing in front of his class and associating with each student. He looked forward to the opportunity of assisting each of his students in whatever way he could. George loved teaching and he had a great love for each of his students. George went about his regular morning activities with a song in his heart preparing for the day ahead. As he left his house he was enveloped in the calm atmosphere of the morning. He was overwhelmed with emotion as his attention focused on the elegant beauty of the eastern sky. The sun was beginning to reveal itself over the horizon sending brilliant colors of gold, orange, pink and red bursting out across a light gray sky from both sides of the landscape as far as the eye could see to the north and the south. It was a gorgeous site. Everything appeared to have the makings of a glorious wonderful day.

As George drove to work that day, he perused his students and their individual strengths, weaknesses and needs. He thought of his concern, love and care for them. He wanted to do what was right for every student and was determined to treat each one equally with fairness and never show any kind of favoritism or partiality. After all, he loved each one equally.

As class began that day, everything was proceeding as normal. Then the unexpected happened. One of the students, Mary, a lovely young woman, raised her hand. As George's attention turned to her, she exclaimed that she didn't feel well and collapsed on the floor. George rushed to her side. He knelt beside her and using his past medical training, grasped her wrist. She had no pulse. She was in cardiac arrest and needed CPR immediately. George was well trained in CPR, but as he glanced around the room, the reality of the situation hit him. Here stood 13 other students that he loved and cared for just as much as he did Mary. He reasoned that he couldn't possibly give CPR to all of them, and it would be unfair to do something for Mary and not do it for the rest of his students. That would be showing favoritism and would not be treating each student equally. At this point he bent over Mary with an ache in his heart and whispered "Mary, I love and care for you. I know you need CPR. I would like to help you, but I love and care for all the other students just as I do for you. It would be unfair and unequal treatment if I give you CPR and not the others. I can't show partiality or favoritism to anyone because I love you all equally."

Do you feel good about George and his decision to not give CPR to Mary because it would not be fair to the other students? Most people would say what George did was absurd. George did not understand the principle that fairness is not giving everyone the same thing; fairness is giving each one what he or she needs. Equal treatment of unequals is inherently unequal. The fact that everyone is in some way unequal demands that if we truly want to be fair, not show favoritism and treat everyone equally, we must treat and give to each individual according to his/her personal and particular needs.

Let's go back to George and his situation for a moment. Let's assume that when Mary had her problem, George did not know how to give CPR; therefore, because of his lack of ability and knowledge, he did not render that life-saving help. Would you say he did not help Mary because he did not love her or maybe it was because he wanted her to die? That, of course, would be ridiculous. Would you blame him for not helping if he did not have the ability to do so? Of course not. In this case, his lack of help would have nothing to do with his desire or willingness to help or his love, care and concern for her. It would be about his lack of ability.

Let's say that due to George's experience with Mary, he became aware of the necessity of being trained in CPR. Therefore, he took the necessary training and became well-trained in CPR procedures, so he would never find himself in that situation again. Low and behold, about five years later, George is in a class when Johnny, another of his beloved students, fell out of his chair in full cardiac arrest. This time George sprang into immediate action. He gave Johnny the CPR needed as the other students looked on. George was able to revive Johnny and save his life. Did George love Johnny more than he had loved Mary or his other students or was Johnny his favorite student? Was George showing favoritism toward Johnny over Mary and the other students? The answer, of course, is no, no, absolutely not! What then made the difference? For one thing, George's ability had changed. His rendering CPR to Johnny and not to Mary had nothing to do with his love or with favoritism or with equal treatment. It had nothing to do with George's desire to help. It had to do with George's ability to help.

Most people never find themselves in a crisis situation where they need to render CPR to save another's life. Yet, as we go through life, we often find ourselves in situations regarding this principle of fairness which has perhaps even greater and more lasting effects with eternal consequences. In our relationships, whether they are at work, church, with our neighbors, social events or family, the principle involved is the same. This principle applies in the dynamics of all relationships and how it is often used or more particularly misused.

First, let's look at the typical work environment. Many, if not most, bosses, supervisors, businesses, and overall systems have an underlying belief that all employees should be treated fairly with equality. There is certainly not a problem with that underlying concept. Of course, people should be treated fairly and people should be treated equally. The problem arises with a one shoe fits all mentality. When a system, business, boss or supervisor decides that all employees should wear a size 9 shoe, because for some reason that has been determined to be the appropriate size; then pressure is applied to force people with larger feet into a small, tight, non-fitting size 9 shoe. This, of course, causes great discomfort which results in pain, suffering and blisters. This almost always affects productivity, work efficiency and, consequently, morale in a negative way.

On the other hand, those with smaller than size 9 feet have the same problem on the other side of the coin. They are forced into shoes that are sloppy and uncomfortable. It becomes very difficult for people to be effective in their work when they are slapping around with their feet sliding back and forth in shoes which are too large for them; therefore, negative effects are produced. It's easy to see the problem. If one believes that in order to be fair and treat employees equally they all must wear the same size shoe, then in fact, it is unfair and unequal treatment to everyone who does not wear a size 9 shoe. In reality, those who do wear a size 9 shoe are being treated with partiality and favoritism. Once again, it is important to remember, equal treatment of unequals is inherently unequal.

A good example of this principle being used in a positive and effective manner comes from a story told by Dr. Norman Vincent Peale. He tells of a man who was very unsuccessful in his employment. This man just couldn't seem to get things together. He simply was not doing a very good job for his company and by all rights, should have been terminated. In most cases, that is exactly what would have happened. The owner of the company, who apparently had a good understanding of the principle we are discussing, called this individual in and had a visit with him. Rather than terminating him, which many employers would have done, he took time to learn about him.

The owner found that this man was being asked to do things in his job that he just simply wasn't able to do well. Perhaps he was not even properly qualified for some of the things he was being asked to do. Now, obviously, the one shoe fits all mentality and the idea that we must have everyone do the same thing in the same way would have demanded this man's termination. This employer was a very wise and kind man and was as concerned about the individual employee as he was for his company. He obviously understood the true principle of equality and fairness and did not look for reasons or a way to terminate this employee, but rather began looking for how he could use this employee's strengths to benefit the company. This employee was very personable, outgoing, friendly and possessed great interpersonal skills. So this wise employer elected to transfer him into the sales department where he could use his skills and talents in a positive and effective manner. Within a short time, this employee became one of the top salespersons in the entire company and maintained that status for many, many years. This decision benefited both the employee and the employer. Once he was transferred to sales, this man was extremely successful. If we were to use the logic that to be fair and treat everyone equally and everyone must do the same thing, it would necessitate transferring everyone in the company into sales. How absurd and utterly ridiculous would that be, yet based on this way of thinking, if we do not transfer everyone into sales, we are not treating everyone the same.

There are many examples of this type of inequality in which I have been involved and personally observed. Let me share a personal experience I had regarding the same principle while teaching at a University. When I was growing up and going through high school, I saw no need to acquire keyboarding skills. At that point in my life, I thought I was going to be a farmer or a mechanic, and therefore, could see no reason to waste my time, as I thought it would be a waste, taking typing classes. Often life sends us in directions in which we never thought we would go. The idea of teaching at a university was the furthest thing from my mind. It took many years and experiences to move me in that direction until one day, lo and behold, I found myself in the position of a university professor. That was a great and marvelous experience, but there was a downside. Even at that point I still had not acquired any type of keyboarding skills.

After a few years, with the onset and prevalence of technology, the University began to provide online classes which made it necessary for the professors in my department to teach classes online, as well as on campus face-to-face. As I began to teach online classes, it became a great struggle. I worked with difficulty as I would search slowly across the keyboard attempting to answer and interact with online students. The fact is I did not do as well with the online classes as I should have. Not because I didn't want to, nor because I didn't care about the students and their education, but because I had a limited capability. On the other end of the spectrum was my face-to-face on-campus classes. These classes were very positive, exciting and productive both for me and the students. Most of the students thoroughly enjoyed my class and commented on how much they learned. I know I was able to give the students valued information and the benefit of personal experience which would help them as they moved into their professional life. Unfortunately, my online students did not receive that same quality of education.

Some of the other professors in my department had strengths which were quite opposite of mine. They really did not do that well in the classroom face-to-face. They were somewhat boring and failed to give the students a very positive educational experience. These same professors, however, were great in teaching online classes. They thoroughly enjoyed teaching online and were able to use technology effectively to give the students a positive educational experience. Understanding this, it made sense to me that I should be assigned to teach all or at least most of my classes face-to-face and other professors who were effective and preferred to teach online classes could be assigned to do so, thereby maximizing my strengths in the classroom and their strengths teaching online.

My department chair, however, was very much into the idea that on order to treat each one equally, it would be unfair to let some professors teach all or most of their classes face-to-face and other professors teach all or most of their classes online. Can you see the one shoe fits all mentality at work here? Because of this erroneous idea of equality, I struggled and suffered personally and my online students did not receive the same educational experience as my face-to-face students. Once again, equal treatment of unequals is inherently unequal. In some way, we are all unequal. It becomes evident that as a boss, supervisor, employer, parent or whatever the case may be, if we truly want to treat people equally with fairness and not show partiality, we need to strive to find what size shoe fits, and provide the proper fitting shoe for each individual.

We see the misuse of this same principle in various settings such as work, families, church, neighbors or social groups. This misuse of the principle results in jealousies, misunderstandings, feelings of hate, etc., and often people become offended, angry, feeling unimportant, unloved, left out and lonely. It doesn't matter what the setting may be, whether in church, social groups of all kinds, among neighbors or wherever we may be. As mentioned before, this principle applies in all relationships. It is important to understand that any interaction with another individual is a relationship at some level. Whatever the setting or the relationship may be, anytime one attempts to treat those involved fairly and with equality by giving everyone exactly the same, that relationship will not function properly. There will be frustration, stress and lack of effectiveness, because many people in that relationship will have shoes that do not fit properly. It is highly important that this principle is understood by all parties involved in the relationship.

Now let's focus our attention to one of the primary relationships in our life, namely the family. This principle of equality, fairness, favoritism, and partiality is particularly important in families. Families are the most important relationship we now or ever will have. Far too often, we see the relationships within family units stressed, damaged and sometimes destroyed because of selfishness, anger, jealousy, greed, and other negative emotions that grow out of feeling mistreated. Siblings often feel that their parents have favorites. They often feel treated unfairly and believe partiality is shown. These feelings often become the foundation for many negative consequences occurring within the family unit. Jealousy, indifference, self-pity, withdrawing physically, mentally or both, result in anger, yes, and even hatred, if these emotions are not checked and brought into submission through knowledge, love, understanding and forgiveness. The ironic thing is that in almost all cases, these negative feelings and emotions are not based in reality.

It is true siblings are treated differently; after all, each individual is different. Each one's needs are different from the other, therefore, in order for parents to treat each child fairly, they must treat each child differently. Parents must give to each child according to the individual needs of each particular child. I don't believe any child would feel mistreated, left out or less loved if a parent were to give CPR to a sibling who was having a heart attack. Yet, when we harbor the negative feelings and thoughts that accompany them because parents may treat one child different according to their need than the other child, we are doing exactly the same thing. It is as if we were to deny CPR to the one child who needs it while the other children who did not need it stand by watching.

There is another aspect to this principle in regards to children feeling unloved, left out, treated unfairly, unequal and different from their siblings. I think I can best explain this with a parable I call the parable of the water bucket.

One day a young man was wandering through a forest when he came upon the most beautiful, glorious tree he had ever seen. It was a very large tree with strong, smooth, yet rugged branches which meandered through the air gradually reaching toward the sky. The large, deep green leaves offered shade and protection to all who would take time to avail themselves of this wonderful gift the tree had to offer. The abundant fruit was large and luscious. This young man desired to have a tree like this for his very own, then his eyes fell upon a beautiful and wonderful sight. There it was, just a little way off, a small but very healthy sapling. This sapling had the potential of becoming just like its parent. He was so excited. Carefully, he dug around the roots in order to remove it without damage. He took great care to protect the roots, as he quickly took his prize sapling home for transplanting. He did his utmost to plant his newfound treasure in the best possible soil. He loved his new tree. He loved it so much he could hardly wait for it to grow to maturity. Now, of course, it needed water and it needed water every day.

The young man was faithful and diligent in caring for his tree. There was, however, a problem. The law of the country in which he lived, demanded that he could only take one bucket of water per day to his lovely little tree. He never missed a day. He would take his five gallon bucket of water and carefully give it to his tree every day, but the tree was not doing very well. You see, the tree needed ten gallons of water per day. In spite of all the hard work, diligence, and love he had for the tree, it began to suffer. Why was the tree suffering? It needed ten gallons of water per day, but it was only receiving five. The problem was not in the young man's desire, love, or concern for the tree. The problem was that his ability to provide the needed water for the tree was limited. He took his five gallon bucket full of water to the tree every day, but the tree needed ten gallons. Unfortunately, a five gallon bucket will only hold five gallons and he was only permitted to take one bucket per day. The fact that he did not give the tree all the water it needed had nothing to do with his love for the tree. It had nothing to do with his desire to provide and care for the tree. It was totally a result of his inability and his limited capacity. The only way he could provide more and meet the needs of the tree would be to increase his capacity.

I suppose there are some parents who are sufficiently evil that they do not care about their children. They have no love or compassion for anyone but, I believe this is rare. Almost all parents care about and love each of their children equally. Most parents do all they can for each of their children based on each child's individual need to the best of the parent's ability and to the extent each parent's capacity allows them to do so. What more can one expect? Can parents be expected to somehow defy the laws of the universe and carry ten gallons of water in a five gallon bucket? That, of course, is impossible. Furthermore, when parents give all they are capable of, is that not 100%, even if it does not fully meet the needs of the child? Remember the widow's mite; her gift was not much, but it was all she had. Jesus declared that she gave more than all the rest.

As children in our family units, it is important that we remember parents are not perfect and often the capacities of parents are limited. Parents' abilities and capacities change with time. Different dynamics within the family unit change as older siblings grow, and younger siblings come along. It is true that children within families are treated differently because the needs of each individual child are different. Many times the treatment differs in order to meet the needs of the individual child. These differences have absolutely nothing to do with the parents' love, care, concern and desire for the well-being for each child. In almost all cases, each child is equally loved and parents are equally concerned for each. When we, as children, understand and internalize this concept, we need to humble ourselves and let go of pride and erroneous negative feelings which may have developed as a result of misunderstood and misguided illusions. The apostle Paul said that when he was a child, he understood and thought as a child, but when he became a man, he put away childish things. We, too, must learn to put away the inappropriate childish thoughts, attitudes and feelings which are based in the limited understanding of a child's mind and allow ourselves to see things as they truly are.

I have addressed only a few specific areas where this principle regarding fairness, equality, and favoritism affects our lives, but it is very important to understand that these principles apply equally and in the same way to all of our relationships with our fellow men. As we move through life and strive to understand and apply this principle, making personal adjustments in our attitude, thoughts and ideas, we will find much greater love, understanding and forgiveness coming into our personal lives which will bring about greater inner peace, joy and happiness in this life, as well as abundant eternal blessings in the life to come. It is my sincere hope and desire that each of us, as members of the human family, may have enough personal character to humble ourselves sufficiently so that we may learn, understand and apply this principle in all aspects of our relationships throughout our life.

Rage

Walking down the hall of a university building can be quite an experience. You never know what you may hear or see. It is not uncommon to see students sitting on the floor with long gangly legs spread across the hall. If you don't watch where you are walking, it is a recipe for disaster, as the students seldom think about moving their legs. In their defense, it may be safe to say they seldom think about much of anything.

Often overheard are parts of very interesting conversations. But by far the most interesting conversations of all are the ones you overhear from professors. I believe there is a great education to be had by listening to and pondering these unsolicited, unprepared, informal conversations. I had an experience which is a great example of this as I was walking down the hall in Rarick Hall one day. Two professors were talking quite loudly. One was obviously very upset. He was expressing how angry he was, using some language I would not include here. I thought to myself, something pretty serious must have happened that was responsible for him allowing himself to become so upset and angry. As I listened to him rant and rave in anger, it became evident what had happened. There had been a meeting scheduled that day which he was to attend. When time for the meeting arrived, he left his office and walked across campus to the meeting, only to find the meeting had been cancelled. No one had bothered to let him know. He was furious. He had taken his time to go to the meeting to find out, upon arriving, there was no meeting.

As I continued to listen to and observe his behavior, I pondered his experience and tried to analyze it as a nonbiased outside observer. The fact that the meeting was cancelled and he was not informed was, of course, not right. The thing, however, that weighed on my mind was how he had allowed this to affect him. From a physical standpoint, there were many negative and harmful things going on in his body. His blood pressure and heart rate were increased. His stomach acids were running wild. His mental reasoning abilities were greatly impaired. He was expressing himself in a way that would not be endearing to anyone who was witnessing his behavior. There was nothing positive to be gained from his anger. In fact, it is quite possible that others would hear him and relationships could be damaged. Often when a person is that angry, the anger is transferred to others who have nothing to do with the issue. He may have transferred his anger to his students. He may have gone home and transferred it to his wife or his children or perhaps a pet, the list could go on and on. All for what?

All the anger he could muster could not change what had happened. The meeting had been cancelled and he was not informed. Right or wrong, nothing could ever change that. It may be true, what happened was wrong, but it did not or could not make him angry. His anger was his and his alone. He chose to become angry because of what happened. No matter what happens to anyone, the anger response is an individual choice. Things do not make one angry People do not make one angry. Circumstances do not make one angry. There is absolutely nothing in our environment that has the power to make us angry. Anger is a response we choose to allow due to some stimulus in our environment. To say this or that made me angry is a cop-out in an effort to avoid responsibility for our behavior.

We, as human beings, can control our anger. We have the power to allow it to escalate until it controls us or we can control and subdue it until we turn it off. The choice is ours. It should be remembered that over time, our anger response becomes a habit and as with any habit, it becomes more deeply imbedded and more of a habit the more frequently it occurs. This habit principle applies in both directions. The more we fail to control and subdue our anger response, the more automatic our out-of-control anger becomes in response to the stimulus we encounter in our environment. On the other hand, the more we control and subdue our anger response to our environment over time, the more our nature and innate character becomes anger free.

I often hear statements like…this is just the way I am, or it runs in my family or they made me so mad, etc. These kinds of statements, whether conscious or subconscious, are nothing more than an effort to shift responsibility from one's self to someone or something. It is simply saying, I am not responsible, you are. Think about it…if God created us without the ability to take charge of and control our anger or another feeling, appetite or passion, then we cannot be held responsible and God would be responsible. That, of course, is not true. We were created and given agency and sufficient power in ourselves to control all of our feelings, appetites and passions, including anger.

I have heard people say, I could not help it; I was so mad. Consider this for a moment. Think of a time when you were very angry, you may have been acting badly, maybe using bad language, yelling or whatever your behavior may have been. Right at that moment when you were at the height of your anger, the phone rang or someone came to the door. Did you go to the door or answer the phone yelling and expressing your anger in the same inappropriate way? Or, did you immediately take charge of your anger, control your behavior and speak more quietly in a much calmer manner with your behavior being appropriate, perhaps even positive. If you can control your anger in this situation, then you can control your anger in all situations. One can never honestly use any excuse for uncontrolled anger.

One simply must accept responsibility for one's own anger. Anger is a normal human emotion. It is not the feeling of anger that is the problem, but the choice to not control it which becomes the problem. Ironically, as with my university colleague, in most cases, choosing to be angry will not change anything and in almost all cases, there is nothing good or positive that will ever come from it. As one chooses to take charge of and control one's anger, the emotion itself weakens and, over time, the anger response to the stimulus in the environment occurs less and less often.

There is a story of an old Indian grandfather who was explaining to his grandson that everyone has two wolves inside. One is a good wolf and the other is a bad wolf. The bad wolf is full of anger, outbursts, bad language, yelling and all manner of inappropriate behavior. Holding to pride and refusing to control his anger, he loves to let it rage. The good wolf, on the other hand, is just the opposite. He is self-monitoring, controls his anger and other emotions, does not use bad language, yell, is not prideful and controls inappropriate behavior. The little boy asked his grandfather if he had both of those wolves inside of him. His grandfather responded that everyone has both wolves inside. With that, the little boy asked which one would win. The grandfather simply said that it is the one you choose to feed.

We all have a choice to feed one wolf or the other. The one we feed will grow and become stronger. The one we starve will weaken and eventually die. We need to continually be aware of which wolf we are choosing to feed.

Each time we allow our anger to rage and control us, we are feeding the bad wolf. As we do this over time, anger and rage grow inside us, becoming stronger and more a part of our inner character. Anger and rage become easy and spontaneous. On the other hand, when we take control of our anger and rage, we begin to subdue it and gain power over it until we become the master and are no longer in bondage. The ability to choose to control our anger and rage become part of our inner character. The principle here is simple. Ralph Waldo Emerson stated, "That which we persist in doing becomes easier to do, not that the nature of the thing has changed but that our power to do has increased."

It's Lonely at the Top

It's lonely at the top. This is a saying which may or may not be familiar to you. I have heard it from time to time throughout my life. It's lonely at the top. Just what the heck does that mean? As I ponder the saying, my mind goes back to a time when I was teaching school. Most people who have had much to do with the public school system know that school secretaries have a lot of power in the school. The principal relies heavily on the secretary and, right or wrong, listens to them to a great extent. This is not necessarily a bad thing, but at times, it can be the catalyst for some most interesting dynamics.

My principal was a good woman and an excellent principal. She always treated me well and was professional in her work. The secretary was also a good woman. I liked her as a person, but her personality was rather assertive. She was very vocal and was always right, at least she thought so. In addition to her personality style, her husband was from one of the old original families in town. That seemed to give her an underlying connection to the community. She always seemed to know everything about everyone. In my experience, when a person knows everything about everyone, that is a recipe for problems.

Due to the secretary's verbal assertiveness, my principal listened to her a lot. I would hear statements from my principal such as, the community thinks or people are saying…. I finally learned to ask who is the community? Who are the people? Give me a name. In most cases, a name was never forthcoming. I found that there may have been one or two things going on. The community/people were usually one or two disgruntled verbal persons or in some cases the secretary's own thinking, which was just projected into the community in her own mind. Hence, I reached the conclusion, if you cannot give me names, facts and details, it is not real. If it is not real, I cannot afford to spend my valuable time and energy with either thought or action regarding this matter. One day my principal was feeling anxious and perhaps overwhelmed as she was dealing with some rather common school type problems. I heard our secretary say, you know, it is lonely at the top. What? I thought. The top? What the heck is the top? She was a principal of a little elementary school of about 160 students. After all, there must have been four or five hundred people living in town. Is that the top? The top of what? I couldn't help but think, if you were in an airplane 50,000 feet in the air, what would our little town look like? Not much!

That experience has been the stimulus for a lot of thinking on the subject. If we follow this through, we must ask the question. What is the top? What does that mean? Where is the top? Also, when we truly find the top, is it really lonely there? Is being principal of a school the top? What about being superintendent? Maybe being the governor is the top. But wait, what about a congressperson or maybe president of the country, or CEO of a major company. Could any of these positions or anyplace in between be the top? Just as our little town becomes insignificant from 50,000 feet in the air, even a country is rather insignificant from a satellite. What would it look like from the moon or from any other planet in our solar system? One cannot even see a country, in fact, the earth would appear only as another planet. If we were to move further out into the galaxy, the earth would not even be visible. Lonely at the top? Who do we think we are? It is my understanding that astronomers estimate there are approximately 400 billion stars of various sizes and brightness in the Milky Way Galaxy alone. Astronomers estimate the number of galaxies in the universe to be between 100 billion and 200 billion.

Beyond this and far beyond these numbers that are too large to even comprehend, all one has to do is stand in the serenity of a calm, dark night and gaze into the heavens or consider the migration of the beautiful delicate monarch butterfly or the various varieties of birds who travel thousands of miles each year with precision and exactness to reach their destination. One can only stand in awe of the majestic beauty of a glorious sunset as it gently rolls across the sky spreading its multiple hues of color along the horizon or when one witnesses and feels the awesome power of a thunderstorm as the lightning bursts through the heavens with an explosion of energy as it strikes the earth, accompanied by an enormous clap of thunder as a witness of its presence. One can only stand with helplessness against the power of a tornado, hurricane, tsunami, or earthquake. The list can go on and on. One can wonder at the miracle of life looking at a newborn infant or the development of the human body with all of its intricate and complex systems, such as nervous, muscular, skeletal, circulatory, immune, digestive, respiratory, endocrine and senses of sight, hearing, touch, taste and smell. What a marvelous creation! A magnificent machine! There is nothing in the world that can even come close to the complexity and wonder of the human body. Add to that the breath of life and we have a living soul, all in a matter of nine months. Is it any wonder that prophets such as Moses, after witnessing in a vision the creations of God, would exclaim "Now, for this cause I know that man is nothing, which thing I never had supposed." (Moses 1:10)

Once again I refer to the question, what is the top? Who do we (people in general) think we are? Do we think we are at the top because of some insignificant position. What a joke! Ironically, there is a top, a true top, and, surprisingly, it is not a lonely place. The world teaches the top to be some worldly position, power or accomplishment and those places can be lonely. People who are caught in the illusion that any worldly position, power or accomplishment is the top should realize they are living a lie. Worldly thinking is fostered by the present ruler of the world. He is the prince of darkness and the father of lies. Anything he promotes may have some truth, but it is intermingled with lies, illusions, and is designed to destroy and keep us from moving forward to reach the true top.

The true top can only be found in one place, which is our Lord and Savior, Jesus Christ. After telling His apostles He would soon be leaving, a discussion ensued as to which one among them would be the greatest after He was gone. Jesus gave a simple answer when He said that he that is a servant of all is the greatest. The true top is obtained as a result of obedience to God and service we give to others. The more we serve and assist others, unselfishly giving love, kindness, patience, long-suffering, etc.; the higher we climb toward the top. This true top is anything but a lonely place. Those we serve grow to love, respect and support us and are willing to stand by us through time and eternity. Another thing happens as we move toward the true top. Jesus said, "Peace I leave with you, my peace I give unto you: not as the world giveth, give I unto you. Let not your heart be troubled, neither let it be afraid." (John 14:27) The peace we receive as we move toward the true top is unspeakable and gives a deep inner peace, joy, happiness and the confidence and security that all is well. There is no loneliness with that feeling. There is a great sense of confidence, security, faith and trust in our Savior. In addition to all this, you like yourself and you can never be lonely when you truly like the one person who is always with you.

Lonely at the top? If the top we pursue is one based on worldly illusions of grandeur, the answer is yes. It is lonely at the top, because this top is not a top it all. It is only an illusion created out of a lie. A lie perpetrated by the father of lies. At the present time, he rages throughout the earth using, among other things, lies and illusions to deceive and destroy. He would have us believe that position, prestige, money, control, and worldly possessions somehow make one superior to others. From a worldly perspective, once we have achieved any of these things, we feel we are moving toward the top. What a lie! It may feel good at the moment, but it is all superficial. It passes quickly, then one is left empty and wanting because no one really cares. Often we have hurt others in the process. This is truly a lonely place. Thus we can say, it is lonely at the top, if that is the top to which we aspire. If this is the case, what an illusion we are under. What a sad lonely place to be.

I Want What I Want

Why? Why? Why? No doubt, this is a question that has run through the minds of many people, along with frustration, anger, and sometimes words that should not have been spoken, as they endure one of life's most trying experiences. The experience to which I refer is the experience of handling animals. It does not seem to make any difference the kind of animal you are trying to handle, whether it is cows, horses, sheep, pigs, goats, and even chickens; the experience is basically the same. Animals do not care what you want or why you want it. They don't even care if it is best for them. All they care about is what they want. They want to go this way or that way. They want to go back or they don't want to go at all. If they see an opening or chance to escape; they will go for it. Why are they that way? The answer is simple. They want what they want and they do not care what you want. I have found it to be very interesting. The harder you try and fight to control and force them to do what you want them to do, the more they resist and try even harder to do what they want to do. I often found myself pushing, pulling and sometimes yelling in an attempt to get the animals to do what I wanted them to do. None of these efforts made much difference. Attempting to handle animals by force almost always ends up being difficult and turns into a frustrating experience.

After many years of pushing, pulling, wrestling and worrying in an attempt to control animals, I finally understood. It is much easier to get animals to do what they want to do and go where they want to go than to try to get them to do what I want them to do by force. No one, including animals, ever resists doing what they want to do or going where they want to go. This is not a new or novel idea, as it has been around forever. The greatest teacher of all, our Savior Jesus Christ, taught this principle many times throughout His life. The principle He taught is that it is easier and more effective to lead and have others follow than to drive, push, control or manipulate. The problem is that most of us just do not understand the principle. It took me a long time, but once I understood, it has revolutionized my life in regards to handling animals. What was once a dreaded chore has become an exciting, joyful and fun experience.

It is no secret that most animals like and want grain. They will fight to get it. I have known that all my life. Yet, it has been only the last few years that I was smart enough to realize I could use their wants and likes to accomplish what I wanted. The ironic thing is that implementing this principle has taken almost no effort on my part. The way it works is simple! I have a small blue bucket I would put a little grain in and take to the animals. From time to time, as I would walk into the field, I would call and whistle to get their attention. Sure enough, they would come to get their grain. They loved it. It was not long until they would see me coming into the field and they would come running. The rewards of that little bit of effort have been phenomenal. I have two horses, a few cows, a bull and a small goat herd.

Animals possess a unique characteristic. They seem to think the grass is greener and better tasting on the other side of the fence. As a result, they occasionally break through the fence and get out of the pasture. Now, I no longer have to chase the animals and try to round them up in an attempt to keep them together by running back and forth, out of breath and frustrated. In the past, I would often have to call for help. When the animals get out, all I do now is take my bucket of grain, find the animals, call and whistle. You guessed it, they come running. I walk with ease back into the pasture where they belong, as they willingly follow along. When I need to move them into another pasture or corral, I simply take my bucket and call to them. They follow me wherever I go. You see, when their needs are being met and they're getting what they want, there is no need for me to drive them because they willingly follow.

One of my steers, who weighed about 1400 pounds, needed to be loaded into my rusty old blue stock trailer. Loading an animal that size can be a problem. Because of my past experience loading animals, I worried about loading this large steer. Before I understood and learned this principle, I had many battles which took time and extreme effort loading animals. Putting this principle into practice, I soon found my worries to be of no concern. I backed the trailer into place, opened the end gate, put a bucket of grain in the trailer and almost before I could get out of the way, the steer was in the trailer looking for his grain.

The last experience I will share is about my big beautiful New Zealand Kiko Buck. He had never been handled and was quite wild when I got him. Knowing I would need to handle and work with him, I decided to activate this great principle. I staked him on a short rope where he had plenty of grass to eat and every day I would take a handful of grain and let him eat out of my hand, while I rubbed and talked to him. It was not long until he would come to me looking for his grain whenever he would see me. Now, several years later, he comes across the pasture to check out my hand, looking for grain. The application of this simple principle has made my life much easier and allowed me to have much more joy and happiness working with the animals.

Maybe you don't work with animals; so you may ask, why do I need to understand this principle? When the Savior spoke about sheep, goats and lambs, He was not really talking about animals. He was talking about people. Since we all interact with people in some way, it is important to understand that this same principle that applies to animals also applies when we interact or work with people. When we try to push, force, manipulate or control people in any way, they resist. They fight, try to turn back and get away from us. It just doesn't work effectively. On the other hand, when we give people what they want and need, we can easily lead them. They will follow. We must be wise and use good sense to effectively use this principle. For example, I personally like fried oysters. In fact, it is one of my favorite foods. What do you think would have happened had I taken a bucket of fried oysters to my goats, horses and cows rather than grain? Would they have followed me? Of course not. They don't like fried oysters. They like grain. They don't care what I like. They care about what they like.

People are no different. They do not care about what I want or need. They care about what they want and need. When I offer them what they want and need, they will respond and follow. It may take a little time, so we must learn patience. If we will review and follow the pattern our Heavenly Father has given, it will work. The Scriptures teach that God commands and waits until He is obeyed. He is patient. He further guides us by saying that we should be kind, long-suffering, using love, gentleness and meekness when trying to persuade.

As we interact with others, if we would remember and implement this guidance and with patience, strive to help them meet their needs, we would be much more effective and find greater personal reward. Individual needs and circumstances vary greatly, but there are a few basic needs which are universal to all people. William James said that "The deepest principle in human nature is the craving to be accepted." Craving denotes a stronger emotion than a mere wish or desire. John Dewey said, "The deepest urge in human nature is the desire to be important." It is necessary that we help people feel important, accepted and appreciated. People need to feel that someone cares. We should let them know that we care about them and what is important in their lives; even if we have no power to change their situation.

Many years ago, I had an experience which taught me this principle with great power. I had been working as a certified hypnotherapist for a few years, which had given me the opportunity to meet and work with a lot of people at a very deep personal level. I had been working with a particular woman on her low self-esteem. She was a well-educated mother of five who had been emotionally beaten down over the years of her marriage. She was faced with an enormous decision. Should she get a divorce? Some months went by as she struggled with that important decision. Her self-esteem improved over a few months and she quit coming to therapy. Months passed. One day I was in my office browsing through my card file of clients when I came upon her name. The thought crossed my mind that I should call and see how she was doing. Acting upon that impression, I called and talked with her for a few minutes. Things were pretty much the same for her. She was still struggling with the same issues in her marriage. In the course of our conversation, I said something to the effect that I didn't have a solution for her and I wished I did, but I wanted her to know that I cared. Our conversation ended and years passed. One day, she brought one of her sons, who was having some problems, to see me. I asked how she was doing and was pleased to learn that her life had improved greatly. As we talked, she referred back to our phone conversation of several years past and expressed thanks with the statement, "You will never know how much it meant to me just to know someone cared."

People need to know we care. People need to know they are okay and we love them for who and what they are. I am not suggesting people do not need to make changes, improve, repent and overcome things that may be wrong in their life. Don't we all? We should remember that in spite of what may be going on in their life, in spite of struggles they may be having, they are children of God and deserve our love, concern and support. Our place is not to judge, but to love and do our best to help them meet their basic needs of feeling accepted and important. As we have more concern about their wants and needs and less about what we want and need, there is no reason to drive, control or manipulate. We can simply guide, direct, teach and wait patiently. This is a better way. After all, this is God's way.

The Dragonfly Syndrome

The cool shade of the front porch gave welcome protection from the heat of the penetrating summer Kansas sun, as my wife, Linda, and I sat in our porch chairs enjoying some together time. The Kansas wind was blowing rather vigorously across the grassy fields. We were not paying any attention to the wind, as it forced its energy around the corner of our house past shrubbery and the crabapple tree, which cuddled right against the end of the porch giving Linda and I ample protection.

Suddenly a dragonfly caught our attention. This little guy was doing his best to make it around the corner of the house. He was working and flying as hard as he could, but unfortunately, he was not making any progress as he was flying directly into the wind. As Linda and I sat and talked, we became more and more interested in this amazing little friend. He just would not give up. After 20 or 30 minutes had passed, he was still there flying as hard as he could, but still no progress. He simply could not make it around the corner of the house. By this time, I had become so intrigued with his determination and yet making no progress, that I began to develop the Dragonfly Syndrome.

I projected my mind into the life of my little friend. I imagined him going home that night totally exhausted. I could see him entering his house, plopping down in front of the TV and telling his family how hard he had worked and had not stopped flying all day long. As he sat back in his easy chair, a sense of satisfaction and pride would sweep across him because of all the hard work he had done. He was unaware this was actually a false sense of pride and satisfaction because all of his work had been to no avail.

There are a number of analogies which can be drawn from this scenario, however, I am going to address one which I feel is of particular importance in our lives. People seem to be so busy. They work hard and run here and there in an effort to meet all the demands of our modern society. Many people work almost endless hours. Sometimes this is due to their own choosing and other times, it is due to the demands of their circumstances. The question is, how productive is all this work? Does it really move them toward their objective or does it just look and feel good? How often are we caught up in the thick of thin things that is sometimes referred to as busy work? In reality, do we go home at night tired and totally exhausted because of all the hard work we have done, not realizing that like the dragonfly, we have accomplished nothing or at least nothing of value? Do we go home after flying hard all day feeling good about ourselves because of the many hard hours we have spent working, when in reality, we have only been flying into the wind and have made little or no progress. It has been said that 90% of our effort is nothing more than busy work, being caught in the thick of thin things, in other words, just flying into the wind and making no progress.

I used to teach my education students at the university that before they gave an assignment to their students or prepared a lesson, they should ask themselves what I refer to as the why questions. Why am I doing this? Will it make a difference? To whom will it make a difference? When will it make a difference? Will it move the students closer to the objective? If these questions cannot be answered in a positive way, chances are what you are asking your students to do is a waste of time and energy; not only for students, but for the teacher as well. We may be busy, that is true, but if we are not moving forward toward our objective, we are like the Dragonfly… flying hard, but going nowhere. That being said, the first thing teachers must do is identify their ultimate objective. If we do not know what our objective is, than it is impossible to reach it. Once we have identified our objective, the why questions will help us know if we are using our time and energy effectively and efficiently to move toward our objective.

This same principle that I taught my students apply to each of us in our personal life. It is important to identify our objective in life. Once we have done that, we can begin to ask ourselves the why questions. In deciding how and where to spend our time, ask the why questions. When we go home at night tired and feeling good about how busy we have been, ask ourselves the why questions. When others place demands on us, ask ourselves the why questions. When we feel all we do is work, eat and sleep, ask ourselves the why questions. We may find that we are suffering from the Dragonfly Syndrome, i.e., caught up in the thick of thin things, involved in lots of busy work, spending our life day after day just flying into the wind going nowhere and never living our life. It is easy to become so busy with life that we forget to live.

An important lesson to be learned from the Dragonfly came as I watched the lack of progress made by this hard working, well meaning, determined little guy. Suddenly, I became aware of another little dragonfly flying close to the ground. He came close to the house and was almost at the same place as his hard working friend. The difference was that he was only a foot or two above the ground. As he approached the corner of the house, he also began to experience difficulty moving forward. He must have had a better understanding of his objective. He obviously understood it is not about the route; it is about reaching our objective. He made a turn, flew out toward the edge of the yard and staying low to the ground, made a gradual turn in his desired direction, and continued on his way until he disappeared from sight. He did not work any harder than his unsuccessful friend; in fact, he did not work as hard. The second little guy made progress and no doubt reached his objective. When he went home that night, he was able to rest in peace and satisfaction, knowing he had truly made progress.

Each of us would do well to ask ourselves often the why questions and considering the answers, make appropriate adjustments in our life. Heaven forbid that we wake up on our death bed only to realize we have flown hard all our life and have gone nowhere, having gained nothing of lasting value.

The Goose in the Wind

The day started out much like most days. My wife had a meeting at the University and needed to be there by 8:30. We raced around getting ready to leave for the 35 mile drive from our country home to the University. It was a nice, calm, beautiful morning. The drive was pleasant and we made it in a timely manner. As we were getting ready to leave, we noticed the weather report on TV calling for a weather front to pass through. High winds were expected as part of this weather front. I dropped my wife off at her meeting and went to take care of some errands around town. The bright sun was beginning to warm the air. As I went from place to place, it appeared that the weather report was wrong. It was a beautiful spring day; however, by the time I made the last two stops, the wind was beginning to blow and was obviously intensifying. I left the last store and drove back to the University. When I reached the university, the sky had become overcast and it was now evident that the weather forecast was most likely accurate. I drove into the parking lot, found a place to park and began to work on a story I was writing. After getting settled, knowing I would be there for an hour or two, I began to think, man, the weatherman was certainly right this time. The forecast had been for 40 to 50 mile an hour winds. By now the winds were that or more. Some gusts were obviously in excess of 60 miles an hour. The truck was shaking from side to side. From time to time, a stronger gust would lift the truck and it felt as though it would come off of the ground.

As I sat thinking about the wind and working on the story, I became aware of three geese off in a distance flying toward me. They caught my attention because of the great struggle they were having trying to reach their objective. The wind was out of the North and they were flying west. I could see the enormous effort they were asserting just trying to maintain their flight path. They came closer and closer to where I was parked and I could tell their objective was to fly to the North. Try as they might, they could not turn to the north as that direction would be directly into the ferocious wind. In fact, using all their effort and flying skills, they could not even maintain a true westerly course. They were slowly slipping further and further to the south, which was further away from their desired objective that appeared to be somewhere to the North.

Their determination was amazing. They were working so very hard, but try as they might and exerting all of their energy, they simply could not make it. By this time, they were almost directly over my truck when they must have realized they had passed their desired landing point. They made a sharp turn to the south. The intense tailwind caught them and they flew over the truck with enormous speed. Making a large circle, they adjusted their course toward the east. This change in their course must have given them a little rest, and most likely their courage and determination increased. They moved eastward still using all their strength, energy and skills to avoid being swept away to the south by the vicious gales. I continued to watch as they made slow, but steady progress. They were fighting hard and making some advancement toward their goal. Little by little they adjusted their flight plan to the north. I marveled at how hard they were working and continued to be amazed at their great flying skills as they fought against this great force of nature.

I had become aware that one goose was flying about 100 feet higher than the other two. The one who was flying higher appeared to be determined to maintain that altitude. The two lower flying geese began to gradually descend until they disappeared from sight behind some trees. The fact that they never reappeared, led me to believe they had landed, finally obtaining their goal. My attention, however, was still fixed on the one who insisted on maintaining his high-altitude. He had reached the point where he was so high and working so hard just to maintain his flight, he was unable to descend to his goal and land with the other two, even though they were right below him. It appeared that his entire focus was on survival. All of a sudden he seemed to throw himself upward in a gesture as if he was exclaiming, this is just too hard. I am through. It is over. I cannot do this any longer, I give up. And that is just what he did. He stopped flying and was immediately caught in the wind and swept to the south at an enormous rate of speed. As he passed in front of me at 50 or 60 miles per hour, I could see that he was making absolutely no effort to fly or to move toward his goal. It appeared that he had not even decided on a different goal; he had not even chosen a lesser goal. He had simply quit and was allowing himself to be carried by the wind. He had given in and was willing to accept and go wherever the wind happened to take him. As I watched, it was only a matter of seconds until he had disappeared from sight miles to the south; miles from the goal and miles from his two friends. As I pondered this amazing event I thought, how often do we as people do exactly that same thing.

When the gales of life blow and the forces of the world descend upon us, all too often we throw our hands in the air and give up. We quit. We say that we just can't do this any longer. We stop flying and allow ourselves to be aimlessly swept away by the winds of life to whatever and wherever they may take us. The sad thing is that often all we have to do in order to avoid this, is to adjust our altitude as the two lower flying geese did. There is no doubt, a great number of reasons why we fail or refuse to adjust our altitude; but whatever the reason, whether pride, fear, ignorance, peer pressure or any other reason, the result is the same. When we adjust, we can excel and move forward toward our goal. When we fail to adjust, we become overwhelmed, feel overpowered, our strength gives out, we quit and are driven aimlessly by the winds of life.

There is a great example of altitude adjustment. The name of John Philip Sousa may or may not mean anything to you, but his story is worth considering. John Philip Sousa lived from 1854 to 1932. He was a famous composer of marches such as Stars and Stripes Forever, The Washington Post, El Capiton, The Liberty Bell March, and many more. Overall he composed 124 marches. He was known as the March King. His marches were played by the Marine band, at the White House and all across the country. There is most likely not one high school band in the nation who has not played one or more of the marches written by this great composer of marches. An interesting phenomenon has been reported concerning John Philip Sousa. At the beginning of his career, marches were not what he wanted to compose. He lived at a time when waltzes were popular and he loved waltzes. He spent countless hours and exerted great energy composing waltzes. The problem was, even though this was a waltz era, Sousa's waltzes did not catch on; his waltzes were not doing well. It appeared that he was not going to ever become successful or famous writing waltzes.

At this time Sousa must have been experiencing great discouragement and frustration. Somewhere along the way, it was suggested that he make an altitude adjustment. It was suggested that he change his waltzes from 3/4 to 4/4 time and turn them into marches. No one knows the work that was required or the personal thoughts and struggles he may have gone through at the prospects of letting go of his beloved waltzes and changing them to marches, but he did just that. The rest is history. Had John Philip Sousa not been willing to make an altitude adjustment, he most likely would never have become famous and the world would never have had his great marches to enjoy.

Each of us face times in our life when it becomes necessary to make altitude adjustments and that adjustment may come in the form of repentance. It may come in the necessity of a career change. It may come as a change in thoughts and attitude. It may come as a change in objective. There are many number of ways in which altitude adjustments may need to be made as we travel through mortality and gain our life experiences. The one **thing** that is for sure, if we are not willing to make those adjustments, we will eventually find ourselves as a high flying goose, out of energy, out of strength, experiencing a loss of will and simply giving up, allowing ourselves to be swept aimlessly by the winds of life to wherever they may arbitrarily take us. If, however, on the other hand, we are willing to make necessary adjustments by letting go of our pride, letting go of our preconceived ideas, letting go of all we might have vested in the direction we are traveling, our burden will become easier and we will have the strength and energy sufficient to move forward in a positive direction. As we do that and listen to the guidance and promptings of the spirit, we will eventually reach our destination. We will fill the measure of our creation and move into eternity knowing we have accomplished our goal, having a sense of satisfaction and accomplishment in completing to the best of our ability those things we were placed on this earth to accomplish. We will be able to say as the Apostle Paul said in 2 Timothy 4:7, "I have fought a good fight, I have finished my course, I have kept the faith."

Any Better Than the Ants

A story is told of five blind men who wanted to know what an elephant was like. None of these men had ever had any association with an elephant. They were very excited about their new upcoming experience. Upon reaching the elephant, one man took hold of the trunk. He very carefully analyzed it, rubbing his hands around and up and down the length of the long, flexible truck. This first man, knowing he had performed a thorough examination concluded, "There is no doubt, an elephant is like a snake."

The second man took hold of the elephant's leg, felt carefully with his hands, wrapped his arms around the leg and reached his educated conclusion, "An elephant is like a tree."

The third man grasped the elephant's tail from the perfect handhold at the base to what seemed to be the poppers at the end of a whip. He reached the decision that the elephant is definitely like a whip.

The fourth man, taking hold of the base of the elephant's tusk, slowly ran his hand along the long, smooth, hard surface until he reached the sharp point at the end. Now he knew that an elephant is like a deadly sword.

The fifth man grasped the elephant's ear. He slowly felt around the edge of the ear, and then rubbing across the ear from side to side, he was certain an elephant is really like a large leaf.

These men left this experience feeling elated, as each one now knew what an elephant was like. There was no question in their minds. After all, they had touched, carefully felt and analyzed the elephant with their hands. As they discussed their newfound knowledge, it became apparent that there was a problem. Although each of them had handled the elephant for himself, they disagreed greatly on what the elephant was like. Each man knew his experience was correct; therefore, what each believed had to be true. They had touched and handled the elephant, yet each of them had a totally different understanding of the elephant. Well, the problem is obvious. Each man was right, but in their rightness, each one became so focused on validating his knowledge that he lost the ability to accept the premise that he was also wrong. Each had some truth, while at the same time; each had a great deal of falseness, misunderstanding and lack of knowledge. The problem was that each man's experience and view was very limited. Each had only experienced a small part of the whole picture.

Growing up in a small Utah town was, for the most part, a great experience. Parowan, my home town, was the first town settled by the Utah pioneers in Southern Utah. It lies about 250 miles to the south of Salt Lake City, Utah. Parowan nestles against the mountains east and south of town. These mountains rise about 10,000 feet like a shadowing giant watching over the town. Over the thousands of years before the pioneers arrived, the water flowing from the streamlets through the mountains and converging in the main canyon, flowed out across the valley creating a large alluvial fan which extended for miles over the valley floor. When the pioneers entered Parowan Valley, they knew they needed to take advantage of the water which flowed from the mountains. They devised an ingenious plan. The valley would be divided into five sections. The town would be one section with the rest of the valley, known as the fields, would be divided into fourths. The water was divided into five parts with one part for each section of ground. In order for the people in town to have water for the yards and home gardens, there were small irrigation ditches dug along the edge of all the roads in town. Water ran through the ditches from early spring to late fall. All property owners were given a water turn of a certain number of hours per week based on how much land they owned. Growing up in Parowan, it was a normal thing to see water running in the ditches through the town.

When I was about 12 years old, my dad decided to plant some trees along the irrigation ditch that ran along the front of our place. I believe they were some kind of poplar tree. Whatever they were, they grew rapidly and as the years passed became enormous. They were in excess of 100 feet in height and measured twelve to fourteen feet around at the base. Many years had come and gone, Mother and Dad had passed away and my wife, Linda, and I were working on the old home. It was a beautiful, warm sunshiny day in early summer. I was leaning against the car, which was parked under one of these gorgeous trees, when I became aware of something I had never noticed before. There were hundreds of little black ants on the tree. As I watched these little guys, I began to marvel. They appeared to be very calculated and definite in their movements. They were scurrying here and there, hurrying up and down the tree as fast as they could. They seemed to have a purpose and good reason for their comings and goings. They were definitely working hard to achieve their objective. I watched them for quite a while. I assumed their journey led them all the way to the top of the tree and back down again. Upon reaching the ground, they would soon start their journey back up the tree.

As I continued to watch this most interesting process, my mind began to project itself into the world of these little ants. To these ants, the whole world must have consisted of this tree. They had absolutely no idea there was anything outside and beyond this giant tree. They were not even aware there were other trees only a few feet away just like the one they were on. In fact, they were so close to the tree, clinging to it in order to climb, they had no awareness they were even on a tree and certainly no concept of how tall or how big around it was. All they were aware of was the soft white bark just in front of their face and the green shimmering leaves fluttering gently in the breeze. From their experience and perception, they must have thought they knew all about the world, yet in reality, they knew almost nothing at all about the world. As the summer rolled along, I continued to watch them and pondered upon this experience from time to time. I marveled at how busy and how hard they were working. They no doubt felt very successful and validated in their work as they scurried up and down, around and around; feeling fulfilled and complete as they were dealing with their world. Little did they know that, in truth, they knew almost nothing about the world. What an illusion they were living under!

Fall came and it was time to return to work at the university where I taught. One day, I was in the copy room making copies for class. It was a fabulous, warm, sunshiny day, much like the day I was watching the ants. As I gazed through the second story window out across campus, I saw many students and a few faculty members going every which way. They were scurrying here and there, some going, some coming. My thought went immediately to my little black ants. Are we (people) really any different than the ants? These students and faculty were very busy (just like the ants). Each had a purpose, objective and (just like the ants) they were working hard. They were scurrying here and there (just like the ants). They were, no doubt, feeling important and validated in what they were doing (just like the ants).

Just like the ants, are we (people) living an illusion? Are we so close to the tree that we miss the big picture? Are we so close to the tree that we have no idea what the world really is? Are we so close to our tree that we do not realize the tree is such a small part of the whole that it is really inconsequential? Are we so involved in the thick of thin things we fail to see the value of truly important things? Are we so busy with life that we fail to live? Are we so close to the forest that we fail to see eternity just on the other side? Are we really any different than the ants as we come and go, scurry about and spend our time feeling important and validated with things that have no true and lasting value?

Our Lord and Savior asked an all important question, " For what is a man profited, if he shall gain the whole world, and lose his own soul? or what will a man give in exchange for his soul?" (Matthew

16:26) As you bustle and scurry through life, day after day, being pushed, pulled and manipulated by the demands and illusions of the world, never looking, searching or reaching beyond to the big picture of eternity, remember the little black ants are doing the same thing. Ask yourself if you are any better or different than the ants. I assure you, in reality, we are not ants and did not come into the world to live at the same level as the ants. We are sons and daughters of Heavenly Father and came into this world to live, grow, develop and improve. We came into this world to learn to be like our Father in Heaven and his son, Jesus Christ, who gave us the perfect example and pattern of life. However, this objective of becoming like Him cannot be obtained by accident. We must work, study, search, learn, apply what we learn, repent and continue to improve. We must hold our objective in the forefront of our minds at all times. If we do not put forth the necessary effort which will lift us to greater heights then we could ever imagine, we will be no better than the ants, scurrying through life, seeking validation from ourselves and others, living an illusion of importance, only to find that we come up short. At some point we will realize that the tree we spent our life on and thought was so important was only a minute part of the whole and we missed the true objective.

The Power of Apology

Relationships are one of the most important aspects of our life experience. As we go merrily on our way, day after day, we form many relationships; it cannot be avoided. When we have anything to do with another person, a relationship develops. Every interaction is a relationship of some kind. There are, of course, many different kinds and depths of relationships, but they are all nonetheless relationships. The quality of our relationships is largely responsible for much of our happiness, satisfaction and success in life. Good relationships tend to bring positive things into our life while bad ones tend to bring negative things. Bad relationships often come back to bite us. My Grandfather Hyatt used to say it is better to have the good will of a dog than the ill will. If you have the ill will of a dog, he may bite you when you least expect it. A great example of this occurred many years ago when I was a young man. We had an old yellow dog named Spot. Spot was one of those once in a lifetime dogs, which most people are never fortunate enough to have. I got Spot as a little puppy from a neighbor when I was 18 years old. He was the runt of the litter and no one wanted him. Over the next few months, he grew and it became apparent he was extremely intelligent. Along with being intelligent, he seemed to want to please; consequently, he learned fast.

Spot was a big pup when I turned 19 years old and left home to serve as a missionary for the Church of Jesus Christ of Latter-Day Saints. When I returned two years later, Spot and Dad had bonded and definitely had developed a great relationship. Dad talked with

Spot just like he was a person and Spot seem to understand and always responded appropriately with one exception. When working with the animals, if Dad would say easy, Spot would go easy. If dad would raise his voice and speak harshly, Spot would become strong, aggressive and hit hard. Spot's response was in direct proportion to the tone of Dad's voice. When dad would say stop, Spot would stop. When dad would say come back, Spot would obey immediately. Spot listened to and obeyed Dad to the letter unless an animal hurt him. If a cow kicked him or if he was hurt in some way, he would get his revenge. One day a cow kicked him hard. Spot rolled across the ground, came up and took off part of the cow's tail. I could tell many, many stories about Spot and how great he was. He was not in any way vicious or mean. Spot was just a wonderful servant.

One day dad and I were at a neighbor's farm combining grain; the man we were working for walked around his truck as spot was relieving himself on a tire, which by the way is what dogs do. The man kicked spot in the side. Spot yelped a little and ran away. That was the end of that, or was it. Later that winter, the same man came to Dad`s shop. After talking with dad for a few minutes, the man headed back to his truck parked in the street. He had just reached the door when, out of nowhere like a bolt of lightning, Spot hit him sinking all four of his large fang teeth deep into the calf of the man's leg. Grandfather's point made! It is better to have the good will of a dog than the ill will. How much, much more important is it to have the good will of people- brothers, sisters, friends, neighbors, coworkers, or even just the passing person that we may or may not meet and interact with again.

Stephen Covey, in his book <u>Seven habits of Highly Effective People</u> addresses rather extensively the concept and value of relationships. He covers a number of principles that go into building and maintaining positive relationships. He talks about the value of the trust level. He also addresses the idea of what he refers to as an emotional bank account. An emotional bank account is just like a regular bank account in which we take withdrawals and we make deposits. Our trust level with another person is in direct proportion to the status of our emotional bank account with that person. The greater the balance in our emotional bank account with another person, the higher the trust level, resulting in a stronger and healthier relationship. There are, of course, other variables involved, but our emotional bank account is one of, if not the most critical, component of any relationship. That being said, it becomes vital, if we care about our relationships, that we understand how to make deposits into our emotional bank account with others. There are many things which are important as we strive to build and maintain a positive emotional bank account with others.

There is one very simple component I have found that is so easy, it almost seems insignificant; but in order to use it effectively, we must be willing to let go of pride. I have noticed that most people do not utilize this great principle very well, even though it has the power to build, cement and enhance every relationship it touches. What is it? The simple answer is apology. Yes! The power of apology. Since I have learned about and began to understand this simple principle, I have used it over and over. Each time I use this principle, the results are phenomenally positive. My experience has proven to me that a sincere apology is beneficial; regardless of the situation or circumstance. Even when you're not sure whether or not an apology is justified, do it anyway. When you know you are in the right and the other person is wrong, what should you do? Apologize anyway. You have to swallow your pride, but the payoff is worth it. Remember that even when you are sure you are right, there is a possibility you may be wrong or at least partially wrong, and the other person most likely feels they are also right.

The truth is, we do not see the world as the world is. We see the world as we are. We do not see ourselves as others see us. It is highly unlikely that we see the entire whole of everything. Therefore, both may be partly right, and both may be partly wrong. Beyond all this, remember when a person believes a thing to be true in his own mind than to him it is true. We must, therefore, address an issue regarding that matter with the understanding that to that person it is true. The facts regarding the actual truth are of little consequence at this point.

A great example of this is an experience I had years ago when I was working as a hypnotherapist. I refer to it as my murder case. A lady in her mid-30s came to my office one day explaining she had a major problem. Her life and health were falling apart. She said that she knew there was something locked in her mind that she just can't get to and it was tearing her apart and she had to find out what it was. At that, I assisted her in gaining a relaxed state and we began the process of unravelling the mystery. During the session, nothing significant appeared, but we must have triggered something on a deep subconscious level. About 2:00 a.m. my phone rang. I answered and this lady said, " I think I witnessed a murder. Can I come and see you tomorrow?" I agreed and the time was set for the appointment. During the session, she saw in her mind a door that she could not open. She knew the answer she needed was behind the door. After about three hours of intense work, she was finally able to open the door. As the door opened she saw a black mutilated body hanging from the ceiling. Once the door was opened in her mind, we were able to work through what she had experienced. Over the following few weeks the mystery gradually unfolded.

When she was about 2 ½ years old it was a time of great racial upheaval and unrest in our country. There were riots and racial crimes and the TV and other news media was filled with reports of violence and demonstrations. A little 2 ½ year old mind is not capable of understanding what is going on, yet emotions and fears may be heightened. One warm summer evening she had been put to bed, but had not yet fallen asleep. The county sheriff, who was a good friend of her father, drove into their yard. The sheriff and her dad went to a building in the back of the yard. After a few minutes, she decided to go see her dad. Getting out of bed, she toddled across the yard to the building and pushed open the door. To her horror, there was a black mutilated body hanging from the ceiling. Her dad quickly picked her up and exclaimed, "What are you doing here?" He immediately took her to the house and put her back in bed. The problem was she had seen what she had seen and a little 2 ½-year-old mind, not being able to understand and deal with the experience, simply locked it up behind a door, leaving her to suffer physically, emotionally and socially through her life.

As we continued to work through this experience, the truth slowly emerged. Her father butchered a lot of animals and it became apparent that he and the sheriff was doing just that; butchering an animal. Her 2 ½ year-old-mind did not understand that, so to her the truth had to do with a hideous murder. To her the real truth made no difference. Her mind and her body responded as if she had, in fact, witnessed a murder. In working through and helping her to solve this problem, we had to approach it as if what she believed to be true was the truth until her mind was re-educated and able to understand and accept the truth. I am happy to report that her false belief was eventually dispelled and replaced with the real truth. Consequently, the problem that had plagued her for over thirty years subsided and she was able to move forward to a more normal, productive and peaceful life.

Most people do not have this type of traumatic experience to deal with, but to some degree, we all have experiences in which we believe a thing to be true, which is not. What we need to remember is, as long as we believe it to be the truth, it is true to us in our own mind. It will remain true to us until information is altered in our mind, enabling us to let go of the false belief and accept the real truth.

Back to the question of why should we apologize, even when we know we are right. Maybe, just maybe we are not right. Remember the other person most likely feels he/she is right. So in the mind of the other person, he/she deserves an apology. Far more important than who is right or who is wrong is the tremendous positive effect on the relationship.

As I have come to understand the value of this principle, I have learned to use it freely. I have never used it without experiencing phenomenal positive results. I had a student in my class who made a statement that was not quite correct. Another student immediately took issue with her. I let them discuss it for a few minutes. It became evident that neither was going to change their thinking. The whole class was listening. It was, therefore, necessary for me to correct the student who was wrong, which I did as tactfully and kindly as I could. As I stated the facts correctly, I noticed her eyes and a slight change in her overall countenance. The next day I met that student in the hall and asked her to come to my office. She came into my office and I told her I owed her an apology. She asked why. I reviewed the classroom experience of the previous day, assuring her that I did not want to make her feel bad in any way. I told her I would never intentionally offend her or cause her to look bad. She replied that it was not a big deal, but she admitted it had bothered her a little. I re-emphasized my apology and concern for her and her feelings. As a professor, did I have a responsibility to correct her misunderstanding and make sure the class had the proper information? Yes! As a professor, did I have the right to say what I feel should be said in class? Yes! But, professor or not, do I have the right to in any way hurt another and not apologize? No! I do not. A noticeable change occurred in the relationship between that student and me. There was a great deepening of trust, understanding and openness that remained throughout the entire semester, simply because I took a moment to apologize.

A co-worker and I, who had become very good friends, met in a store. As we visited, I proceeded to give her some of my great wisdom. The things I told her were good and correct principles and she agreed. The problem is, since I am retired I have the time to do things in a way that working people may not be able to do. As I thought about this overnight, I realized that I may have come across arrogant, all-knowing, and maybe even a little condescending. The very next day I made a point to go to her office. I told her that I owed her an apology as I felt that yesterday I may have come across arrogant and perhaps condescending in telling her what she should do, as I know nothing about her life and circumstances. She assured me that she had not even thought about it, but still thanked me for caring enough to express concern. Once again, another layer of concrete was laid and cemented together in our relationship.

Since I have learned the power of this principle, I use it all the time. I look for opportunities to express apology even if I don't think it is really needed because the results are so fantastic. No one is ever offended with the statement, "I think I owe you an apology." The power that comes from that simple statement is phenomenal. As I said before, it is perhaps the single most powerful tool you will ever find in building and maintaining relationships. I should mention that it is crucial that your apology be sincere and comes out of true concern for those with whom you interact. I challenge you to watch for an opportunity to sincerely apologize to someone. Do it and see what happens. You will be amazed at the power you have and how easy it is to use. I promise goodwill will increase, and after all, it is better to have the good will of a dog than the ill will, and how much more valuable and important is the good will of another person.

The Greatest Battle Ever Fought

Wars, battles and struggles of every kind and on every level are part of the world in which we live. This world has been plagued almost from the beginning of mankind with war: nation against nation, tribe against tribe, family against family, sibling against sibling, race against race, neighbor against neighbor, husband against wife; the list goes on and on. Without exception, these wars, battles and struggles have reaped havoc. They have been the cause of pain, suffering and misery, sweeping across the earth as a great never-ending storm. It is impossible for tongue or pen to adequately address the devastation which occurs, whether it is a world war, a battle between two individuals or any other conflict.

There is one battle which is of greater importance and looms above all others. It has greater potential devastation with far-reaching and lasting effects than any of the other battles. The ironic thing about this battle is that every human being must fight it. One cannot hide, run away, refuse or ignore it. It is impossible to avoid; there is no exception. What is this all imposing battle that we all must fight? It is the battle fought within the confines of our own mind.

There is a story of an old Indian grandfather who was counseling his grandson. This grandfather wanted to give the precious little boy some guidance and direction which would be of great value as he progressed through his life. Grandfather explained that everyone has two wolves inside. One is a good wolf and the other is a bad wolf. The bad wolf is full of evil. He is angry and hateful. He is consumed with jealously and greed. He is a liar, deceitful and unforgiving. He is immoral and sneaky. He is dishonest and selfish. He is unhappy and wants to hurt and make others unhappy also. He is full of pride, self-centeredness and self-gratification. He is full of darkness and evil of every kind. He is a blamer and blames others and the environment for everything that happens and never accepts responsibility.

The good wolf is just the opposite. He is full of love, understanding and tolerance. He is kind and forgiving. He is selfless and thinks of others even before himself. He is helpful, uplifting, loves to serve others and help them become happy. He is full of virtue and longsuffering. He is honest and truthful in all he does. He is humble, meek and gentle, while at the same time, he is strong and firm in his convictions and faith. He loves light and truth and seeks goodness and right. He exercises self-control over his emotions, passions, appetites and desires. He is calm and peaceful and thinks before he acts. He is active, not reactive. He chooses his actions and takes responsibility for them. He does not react and then blame others.

The Grandfather explained that these two wolves are always fighting each other and one will eventually win. The little boy asked, "Grandpa, do I have both of those wolves inside me?" The wise old grandfather responded, "Yes, my son, everyone does." The little boy's big brown eyes were wide, full of concern and a little fear, as he looked deep into the old dark eyes of wisdom surrounded with the deep wrinkles of time and experience in his grandfather's face and asked, "Which one will win?" The answer came in four all powerful words, "The one you feed."

We live in a world of cause and effect, of absolute laws which never vary or change. Gravity always works; electricity always does what electricity does; plants always reproduce after their own kind; element put together or taken apart in a given way will always respond in the same way. The bottom line is simple. There is a law that governs all things, and that law applies to all aspects of our mortal life. The law of the internal wolf says, "If you feed it, it lives, if you starve it, it dies." That is what the old grandfather was telling his grandson.

An ancient American prophet, King Benjamin, put it this way, "The natural man is an enemy to God, and has been from the fall of Adam, and will be, forever and ever, unless he yields unto the enticings of the Holy spirit, and putteth off the natural man and becometh a saint through the atonement of Christ the Lord, and becometh as a child, submissive, meek, humble, patient, full of love, willing to submit to all things which the Lord seeth fit to inflict upon him, even as a child doth submit to his father." (Mosiah 3:19)

When we think about feeding or starving the wolf inside each of us, our thoughts tend to turn to what we may think of as big things. It is quite easy to understand that if we allow our thoughts to focus, harbor and work on evil and sinful things, such as committing a robbery, having an affair, lying, deceiving, pornography, adultery or even murder; we are feeding the bad wolf. It is critically important to realize that thoughts which some would view of lesser concern are just as dangerous. When we hold in our mind, think about and ponder seemingly little things, we are still feeding one of the wolves. When we do this over time, the wolf we feed grows and gains more and more power. Even though it may seem small and insignificant, the everyday little thoughts, whether appropriate or inappropriate, do have an impact, as they feed either the good or the bad wolf. Thoughts are like a bird flying over our head. A little anger flies by; maybe it's jealousy, greed, selfishness, immoral thoughts, deceit, envy, etc. Do we invite them in to build a nest by expanding, adding to, pondering, imagining and visualizing? If so, we are feeding the bad wolf. On the other hand, we can change those thoughts by calling in the bird of goodness, purity and virtue and helping it to build its nest which feeds the good wolf. You see, it is really a choice we make and direct in our own mind.

When we left the presence of our Heavenly Father and came to this earth, we took on a physical body and became a mortal being. Due to the fall of Adam, as mortal beings, we become by nature, carnal, sensual and devilish; desiring and craving things of the world; i.e., power, fame, money, control and gratification of the flesh, etc. This is the bad wolf inside of us. Our spirit, however, being Godly and coming from the presence of Heavenly Father as his spirit child, is by nature good and desires to be like Heavenly Father. This is the good wolf inside of us. These two wolves that live inside each of us are always fighting to see which one will win. This fight goes on in our thoughts, our desires and our attitudes, which automatically results in our actions. The outcome of this battle eventually determines our character and the person we are in the innermost depths of our soul.

Because this battle which goes on within the confines of each human mind is so important, Heavenly Father has given us the power to overcome. The one thing, and I believe the only thing, Heavenly Father has given each of us is total authority and control over what goes on in our mind. We can choose our thoughts, our attitudes and desires. The choice is ours. However, the consequences based on these choices are fixed. Our eternal destiny will be based on the result of the outcome of this battle. What we become and who we will be for eternity will be in direct proportion to the result of this all important battle.

The battle that each human must fight is no doubt the most important battle that will ever be fought in this life. It is the most difficult of all battles; yet, at the same time, the victory is easy and simple to achieve. The victory will go to the wolf we choose to feed. Remember, feed it, it lives; starve it, it dies. The choice is ours. We choose each moment of each day to feed one wolf or the other. The one we consistently feed grows and becomes stronger and stronger. As it grows, it demands more and more food and it slowly creeps throughout our soul, becoming more and more a part of us until it entirely integrates our whole being and overpowers the other wolf. Once this has happened, we are no longer at war. We have become either the good or the bad wolf. That is who and what we are and will remain, whether in life or in death. We will be what we have become as a result of the wolf we have chosen to feed. We need to continually ask ourselves which wolf am I feeding. May we always choose wisely and liberally feed the good wolf as we starve the bad one.

Just Short Of The Mark

There is a calm security of peace filling the air. It is a beautiful bright day. Everything seems to be perfect. There is no reason to feel anything short of wonderfully perfect as you assess your life. You allow your mind to ramble back through time as your life events, actions, thoughts and feelings are processed one at a time. Yet, almost instantly, as if they were reoccurring before your eyes, you become aware of those times when your behavior was not as it should have been.(Behavior here refers to feelings, thoughts and actions.) Fortunately, there were many, many times when your behavior was good, right, and as it should have been. There is an underlying anxiety as these scenes flash across your mind.

Suddenly your name is called. It is your turn. Even though you feel an overwhelming sense of love and security, the anxiety within you grows and intensifies as you step forward. The calm, but penetrating voice says it is your turn to step on the scale and be weighed in the balance. You look at the perfectly balanced scale before you with a balance beam extending from side to side. You step forward with hollowness in the pit of your stomach. Now your anxiety begins to intensify and fill your entire body. There is a lump in your throat. It has grown so large that your voice is almost totally impaired. You slowly move forward in order to step on your side of the scale. As you step on the scale, the foremost question on your mind is…. will the scale stay balanced or will I be found wanting?

As I think of the prospects of this future experience, my thought goes back through the years to an early Sunday morning in Eureka,

Nevada. The day started out pretty much like every other Sunday at that time in my life. My family and I had awakened early, eaten breakfast and were ready for church. We got in the car and drove the nine miles to the little meetinghouse, just as we had done each Sunday since we had been living in Eureka. During one of the meetings, the phone rang. In answering, I heard a man's voice on the other end. He said he and his wife were traveling to the east coast by bike, but had run out of money. They had no food and asked if the church could help them. I talked with him for a few minutes and found that they were camped in a tent just outside of town. I explained that I had no authority for the church, but I would talk to the Bishop, who is the designated ecclesiastical leader of our unit, and see what could be done. I talked with the bishop about them and their situation. The bishop said there was nothing he could do because they were transients and because of that, they would have to go to the transit bishop in Elko.

One of the bishops in Elko had the assignment of caring for and assisting transients who were passing through the area. It was obvious to me that these people were in no position to get Elko which was one hundred and ten miles away. I thought about them during the rest of our meetings and wondered what I could possibly do to help them. After church, I decided to take my boys and drive up to the place where they were camped and see if we could help in some way. When we got there, a long-haired unkept, unclean man came out of the tent, followed by a homely, very rough-looking woman. I had to look twice to even be sure that she was a woman.

We talked with them for little while and found that they had not had anything to eat that day. The Sheriff's Department had given them a meal the day before, but that was all the Sheriff could do for them. They told us that they were going to ride their bikes back east to see this man's mother, but did not realize how hard it would be. They found themselves in the middle of Nevada; out of food, out of money and did not know what to do. This man, who I will call Bill, which is not his real name, was feeling very destitute and did not know where to turn or how to proceed. After talking with them. I decided to take them home and give them something to eat. We loaded their tent, bikes and the few meager possessions they had into the back of my truck and took them home.

At home, we invited them to eat Sunday dinner with us. It just so happened, whether by coincidence or not, I'm not sure, that we were planning to travel to Kansas City that week in order to help our oldest son, Andrew, and his wife, Clarice, move there for Andrew to attend medical school. As we talked and become better acquainted with Bill and his wife, we could see that they were good people. They just had a lot of problems. We explained that we were planning to take a trip and help our son move to Kansas City that week and invited them to travel that far with us. We explained that we could haul their bikes and few belongings and that would get them at least part of the way across the country. Bill said if he could even make it as far as Denver that would work. Bill had an uncle living in Denver and thought he could stay with his uncle and get some work to earn money before they continued on their trip.

As mentioned before, this was on a Sunday. The next day we had doctor appointments in Reno, Nevada which is about 240 miles west of Eureka. We told them we would not be leaving on the trip to Kansas City for a few days, as we had to go to Reno to our doctor appointments Monday. Afterwards, our plan was on Tuesday and Wednesday to load up our truck, get everything ready and leave early Thursday morning. We invited them to stay with us until we left for Kansas City. We had a recreation room on the back of our house, so we fixed them a bed in the room and spent the next few days together.

This became one of the more choice experiences of my life. I will never forget it. Sunday evening my wife, Linda, who has been the family barber throughout our marriage, was giving haircuts to me and the boys. Bill asked if she would mind giving him a haircut, as it had been a long time since he had had the opportunity to get it cut. His hair was down to his shoulders. I thought his hair was long like that because he was one of those men who liked long hair. Linda started cutting his hair and asked how much he wanted cut off. His reply was to cut it short, as he didn't like long hair, but he had not had the money to get it cut for a long time. After his haircut was finished, we invited he and his wife to have a shower. After they had showered and gotten some clean clothes on, they thanked us and exclaimed how good it felt to be clean once again. Our daughter-in-law, Clarice, who is quite talented with women's hair, asked Bill's wife if she would like to have her hair done. She was extremely excited about that idea, so Clarice went to work fixing her hair. We witnessed a wonderful transformation. After Bill's hair was cut and he was showered and dressed in clean clothes and his wife showered with clean clothes and having her hair fixed, they were nice-appearing people. They really didn't look anything like they had a few hours earlier when they came out of the tent. At this point, I began to learn a great lesson. I expect many times people's appearance, or lack of cleanliness and their outward appearance, upon which we make judgments, are not a result of their choosing, but are many times the result of circumstances and conditions beyond their control.

Upon returning from a doctor appointment in Reno the following day, we began loading and making preparation for our trip. Finally, Thursday morning, we were ready to get on our way. What a sight to behold, as our little caravan headed down the highway toward Kansas City about 1200 miles to the east. I led the way in my old Dodge truck which was loaded to the brim. Bill and his wife rode with me with their bikes, tent and what few belongings they had tied on the back of the truck. My son, Ben, followed me in our Plymouth Voyager van packed as full as it could hold. Linda and my son, James, were in our old Ford Taurus station wagon. After that came my son and his wife, Andrew and Clarice, in their little Isuzu pickup truck.

We slowly made our way across a high Nevada desert with a top speed of about 50 mph. Grinding along on the old two-lane highway over hill upon hill, around turn after turn, progression was slow, but sure. Hour after hour, mile after mile, we moved forward toward our destination. I had nothing to do but talk and listen. As the hours passed, I learned a lot about Bill and his wife. Bill told the most outrageous and far-fetched stories I have ever heard. His stories were about himself and the wonderful great things he had done and experienced. His wife just listened quietly and patiently. Bill stories were so far out, they could not possibly have been true. It was obvious that his wife knew they were not true. I thought to myself, why does she listen to all those stories when she knows they are not true and she says nothing?

As I thought about this question, the answer began to be clarified in my mind. Bill's stories were not hurting or doing any harm to anyone, but they did help him feel better about himself and feel important. On the other side of the coin, I became aware of how Bill met his wife's needs. Bill's wife was, without doubt, the most homely woman I have ever seen. She told me of times she had been accused of being a man while in the women's restroom. Bill, however, must have seen the beauty in and about her that other people did not see. He was continually telling her how beautiful she was and how wonderful she looked. As I began to learn more about her, I realized she was a very intelligent, kind, and good and was truly a beautiful person regardless of her physical appearance. As this understanding began to clarify, I realized that she was meeting Bill's need for feeling of importance and no harm was being done. At the same time, Bill was meeting her need to feel valued and beautiful as a woman.

We made our way across the Great Salt Flats of Northwestern Utah. After hours of travel, we approached Salt Lake City, Utah. We stopped for gas and a few snacks. Linda and I were financing the entire trip as our son, Andrew, having recently completed his bachelor's degree and not having much money, needed our assistance in making this move. Linda and I had sufficient for everyone to make the entire trip and to help Andrew and Clarice get set up in Kansas City. We, of course, bought snacks and drinks for everyone, including Bill and his wife, as we knew they did not have any money at all. We were in the process of buying snacks and soft drinks for Bill and his wife when Bill said that he had some money and could pay for their food and drinks. That kind of blew me away, as I thought they did not have any money. As I was trying to sort this out in my mind, Bill said that the strangest thing happened. Continuing, he said when he and his wife were rolling up their sleeping bag that morning, they found $37.00 in it. They had no idea where it had come from. At that point, Linda and I had no idea where it had come from. I did learn another important lesson which I believe applies to most people. It seems to me that most people want to be independent, self-sustaining and pay their own way. When they don't, it is due to the fact that for whatever reason, they do not feel able. The mystery of the money was solved a little later. Upon inquiry, our youngest son told us that he had emptied his piggy bank and hid the money in Bill's sleeping bag.

Continuing on, we started our journey crossed the dry, desolate wind-blown plains of Wyoming. Each time we would stop to eat or get snacks or drinks, we included Bill and his wife and paid for everything as if they were part of our family. I was feeling quite good about myself, maybe even a bit prideful. We were doing exactly what the Savior has taught us to do. We took Bill and his wife and gave them food and shelter and was helping them across the country. Cheyenne, Wyoming is about 90 miles north of Denver, Colorado. Bill insisted that rather than continuing on to Kansas City with us, they would take their bikes and ride down to Denver to his uncle's place. The next morning we went our separate ways; they headed south toward Denver on their bikes, and we headed east toward Kansas City. We have not heard anything concerning them from that time on. Is it any doubt I felt good about what we had done to help Bill and his wife.

Now, however, as Paul Harvey would say, here is the rest of the story. Going back to the night we arrived in Rawlins, Wyoming. It was about 10:30 or 11 o'clock. We were all very tired, as we pulled into a motel. I went in and purchased rooms for Linda and I, our sons, Ben and James, and Andrew and Clarice. I came back into the parking lot where everyone was waiting, got our things to take into the motel and told Bill and his wife they were welcome to spend the night in our truck, which they did. The rest of us went into the motel, showered and went to bed in nice comfortable beds.

As the years have passed, I have thought many times about this experience. I have asked myself why didn't I buy a motel room for Bill and his wife. Unfortunately, I don't have a good answer. Even though we were still early in our trip and I had spent quite a bit of money, I still had sufficient to make the trip and do what needed to be done. I have thought about the parable of the good Samaritan. When he found the man alongside the road, who had been beaten and robbed, he stopped to help, even though others had passed him by. The Samaritan cleaned and bound his wounds, took him to an inn and cared for him. The good Samaritan paid for his care and told the innkeeper to continue caring for him and he, the Samaritan, would pay for any extra cost his next trip. He not only began taking care of the wounded man, but he also finished the care. The Samaritan completed the full course from beginning to end.

In my case, I did many things much the same as the Samaritan, but there was one main difference… I stopped just short of the mark. It is as if I ran a good race and just as I reached the finish line, I stopped running. Hopefully, we may all learn the lesson taught by this experience. How sad and painful it would be as we step on the scale of justice, as one day each of us will, to find to our horror and despair that in spite of all the noble, good and great things we have done, the scale didn't quite balance, only because we stopped just short of the mark.

www.ingramcontent.com/pod-product-compliance
Lightning Source LLC
LaVergne TN
LVHW011728060526
838200LV00051B/3078